SHARKS
AND
MINNOWS

Book One of the Jolie Chronicles

ALSO BY E. F. WINTERS

MEMELOOSE: the Island of the Dead
First in category winner
Somerset Awards
Chanticleer Writing Competition

THE PEOPLE'S GIFT

Watch for:

Book Two of THE JOLIE CHRONICLES
GHOSTS IN THE GRAVEYARD

THE KEEPERS OF THE TRUTHS
Book One: EBULON

SHARKS AND MINNOWS

BOOK ONE OF
THE JOLIE CHRONICLES

E.F. WINTERS

Kenspeckle Productions

2013 Kenspeckle Production, LLC

Published in the United States by Kenspeckle Productions, LLC
Distributed by Lightning Source
as Print on Demand and as an e-book

Library of Congress Cataloging-in-Publications Data
E.F.Winters & Kenspeckle Productions, LLC
ISBN 978-1-940531-00-7
Printed in the United States of America

Book design by E.F.Winters & J.L.Winters

CHAPTER ONE

Sunny Las Vegas; yeah, right; sunny and freezing with the wind chill factor of a human icicle. Jolie didn't care what her mother's boyfriend thought, she and her mom lived here; he didn't. The single-wide trailer they rented might be a piece of crap, but it was still warmer inside than it was outside, and she wanted in. She jumped up and down blowing into her cupped hands as if she could capture the warmth from her breath and hold on to it, then took out her cell phone and punched in her mom's number. Jessie was at work and couldn't pick up unless she was on a break, but there was always a chance Jolie would get lucky. She didn't, and her mother's voice mail kicked in.

"Call me or call Rick. I'm locked out of the house and he's still got my key."

A string of pathetic Christmas lights popped on at the trailer next door; the old fashioned kind that made everything look like a circus wagon. Scarred and chipped, like everything else in the run down trailer park, they hung in messy curves and loops, forcing the misery of the place back all of two inches. There had to be a better way for people to brighten their hopeless lives, but if there was, she didn't know anything about it. Hope was something that, at fifteen, Jolie Figg had given up on. She scanned the bruised and beaten trailers.

"God, I hate it here."

The "good life in Las Vegas" lie was just one more in a long line of failed schemes her crazy mother had put them through. Jolie had been there for the birth and death of so many, that she'd given up counting. Once upon a time, she had even believed her mother knew what she was searching for and that they would find it together--but no more. Jessie Lynn Figg was not going to be able to make her life better, and no one else, no matter how much they loved her, could fix it for her. The best Jolie could do now was hold on until she was eighteen. It might feel like abandonment.; it might feel like a betrayal, but it was survival.

It was a cold sunny day; the third week of December, almost Winter Solstice; the shortest day of the year. Not that it mattered much in a city whose glow could be seen from outer space.

"Las Vegas is the brightest spot on the planet," Jolie's mom had told her like it was a big selling point for them to move there. Some geek had actually done a study. After four and a half months, Jolie had the results of her own study; Las Vegas sucked. Its mad addiction to bling was a classic case of overcompensation--like small guys who drove souped-up muscle cars. The city was a playground for the rich and those pretending to be rich, but for people like her and her mom, it was just hot and boring. Except in the winter when it was cold and boring.

Along with the shortest day of the year came the longest night, and though Solstice would come and go without most people even noticing. Its approach always made Jolie a bit blue since its ancient importance had been buried under the newer traditions of its usurper: Christmas.

As a little girl in New Orleans, her grandmother, Mem Boulet, had told her about how ancient people used to stay up all night celebrating the holiday, telling stories and feasting, believing their actions would entice the sun to return--like the sun was just going to keep on going like a deadbeat dad, leaving the world in darkness. But

Chapter One

Mem had kept the old tradition, throwing a huge all night party in her grand old New Orleans house.

Of course, nobody worried about stuff like that anymore. Most people didn't even know the history of the odd date on the calendar; it was just another shopping day before Christmas. Even so, it seemed like something deep inside made people instinctively want to push back the darkness by adding some light to their lives this time of year.

Jolie hugged herself as the sun sank behind the Spring Mountains that bordered the valley to the West. The chill in the air sharpened, and her anger rose. Turning, she banged on the door again, rocking the trailer on its flimsy blocks. Rick would have to be dead not to hear her.

"Open up or I'm calling the cops," she shouted.

She wouldn't of course. Whatever he was doing, chances were her mother was doing it with him, even at four-thirty in the afternoon on a work day. It wouldn't be the first time Jessie Lynn Figg had skipped her shift to hang out with some jerkwad or the first time she'd get fired for it, but chances were if Jolie called the cops Officer Wrangler from Juvenile Probation would show up and she'd be the one who got locked up. Still, a person could only take so much.

"Okay. That's it." Jolie dropped her backpack, jumped off the step and headed for the rusty storage shed in the back. The sign out front of the trailer park boasted that each site had its own private storage--like storing their many worldly possessions was a big deal to residents whose monthly income was lower than most peoples' car payments.

Jolie pushed the dented shed door open a few more inches. It made a terrible scraping sound then stopped, unable to open any further. It wouldn't shut all the way either; a victim of domestic violence or a D.U.I, no doubt. Jolie turned sideways and slipped in.

"Scorpions and spiders get out of my way, cause if I see you, I'm coming back with the biggest can of bug juice I can find," she warned, kicking her way through the half-packed cardboard boxes. It was all stuff she and her mom hadn't needed since they'd moved here, and that would probably be ruined before they needed it again, but somehow it had gotten labeled "to keep" during the last move and escaped the Goodwill pile. Jolie took a breath and gagged.

"Oh God, it smells like something died in here." Holding her nose, she reached up onto the top of the rusty metal shelving left by a previous tenant, and began feeling around for the tin can she knew had to be there. She had it in her hands when a dark figure rose from the shadows behind the door.

"Ah!" She dropped the tin, instinctively grabbing the amulet hanging around her neck. The key inside the tin clattered onto the concrete slab.

The figure froze half lit by the reflected light of the brightest spot on earth.

"This traffic report is brought to you by...." Jolie recognized the old Power Rangers blanket from one of the boxes, now wrapped around the shoulders of an old woman who hung around the trailer park.

"Shit." Jolie let go of the amulet and let out her breath, lifting her sweatshirt to her nose. "You scared the crap out of me. Didn't I tell you not to sleep in here anymore? If Rick or any of his ghoul-friends finds you in here, who knows what they'll do; probably sacrifice you to the shit-faced god of pubic hairs or something."

"Watch out for a four-car pile-up at the Spaghetti Bowl..." The homeless woman muttered; her eyes unfocused.

Chapter One

"Look, I'm not mad at you or anything. You just scared me, but I'm serious, Rick's not a nice person. You can keep the blanket. Take whatever you need it's just junk, but you need to go." Jolie turned the poor thing around, nudging her toward the door.

"Damn!" She pulled back her hands like they'd been burned. The moment she'd touched the old woman, an image of someone beating her had flashed in Jolie's mind. She sucked in a cold breath and tried to steady herself. She hated it when this happened, and it was happening more and more now. When it did, it felt like she was there, looking through the other person's eyes, feeling their feelings. *Jolie couldn't see the attacker's face, because his victim couldn't, but she could feel his anger and she knew, as the old woman did, that this man would not stop. He liked to hit things and he would keep on hitting her until the last glimmer of life had left her body. In the background of the vision, someone was frantically calling the attacker's name, trying to get him to stop. Jolie couldn't make sense of the words any more than the old woman could.*

Flashes of the homeless woman's younger life were spliced between the images of the attack; like how people say your life plays before your eyes just before you died. The old woman had one clear thought: "They'll never know."

Jolie looked past the broken door. The homeless woman stood there staring back at her.

"I mean it," Jolie said, without conviction. "Don't come back here. It's not safe." Looking like a Power Ranger wrapped hot dog with skinny chicken legs, the blanketed bundle shuffled off, mumbling the weather report, through the six by six squares that park residents called their back yards. Jolie watched until the woman went into another shed, then turned back to search for the tin and the key.

"What next?" Jolie hated the fact that she saw private things about stranger's lives. It made her feel like the worst kind of peeping tom, but it wasn't like she did it on purpose. She had no control over the gift--or curse, or whatever it was. It just happened. The only thing she knew to do to keep it from happening, was not to touch anyone, and not to let them touch her, but that only worked part of the time. Sometimes lately, all she had to do was walk by someone and she knew every crummy thing about them.

As Jolie felt for the key on the floor, a shadow blocked the fading light from the door behind her.

"I told you not to—." Jolie started to pull her sweatshirt up to her face again when the unmistakable masculine scent of men's cologne and gasoline reached her nose.

"Hey, gorgeous, what're you doing in here?" a mocking baritone asked.

Jolie stood up and turned around fast so Sean wouldn't be looking at her butt. Too late: his gaze rose from where her ass had been, up to meet her eyes in an admiring taunt.

"I didn't scare you, did I?" His voice was buttery smooth and too sexy for anyone's good; especially hers.

"No," she lied.

"You sure? Cause you look like an extra from the Night of the Living Dead with your eyes all bugged out like that."

"Yeah, right, cause I'm so pasty white." Whenever she started at a new school, which was at least once or twice a year, Jolie had to go through the mandatory "are you one of us" routine while people tried to figure out who and what she was. With skin the light creamy tones of heavily doctored chocolate it was hard to tell.

"You're a little bit of everyone who came to New Orleans and made it their home," Mem had explained once when Jolie had asked about their family background. *"Chitimacha, French, African, Acadian, Irish, and more than a little Spanish. New Orleans was multicultural before people had a name for it, and our family has roots all the way back to the original people who settled here; the Chitimacha Natives."*

Jolie frowned as she pushed her pink streaked brown hair out of her eyes.

"You shouldn't sneak up on people, Sean."

"Sorry." He smiled, unfeigned by her false show of ferocity.

Sean Flahretty was about the only thing Jolie did like about Las Vegas. Trouble was, she liked him too much, and she was pretty sure he liked her too much, too. She hadn't asked, but he had to be at least twenty-four and that made her jail bait, even in Nevada. She tried to ignore the full bodied scent of him and the way his liquid blue eyes made her feel all soft and melty.

"Where's your bike?" Sean not only dressed in the "rebel without a care" style of a biker, he had the machine to back it up.

"Over at The Well. Rick and I were gonna get a couple of drinks, but he said he wanted to drop in on your mom before she went to work. Haven't seen him since." He gave Jolie a knowing grin. There weren't very many things two people could do in a nineteen-eighty-seven single-wide trailer.

"I don't know which would be worse, him dropping in for a quickie, or him getting her high before she has to go to work," Jolie said bitterly.

Sean shrugged. "I just came to see what was keeping him. Just my luck, I found you instead." His eyes sparkled like he'd discovered buried treasure and she was it.

Jolie's cheeks felt tingly and warm, and they weren't the only places. The way he looked: sandy brown hair brushing his cheeks, tight buns, and a cover-boy face; he would have been hard to resist if he'd talked to her like she was an idiot, but he didn't. Sean actually treated her like a real person, not just Jessie Lynn's kid. That made him even more attractive and therefore even more of a problem.

"Rick's inside," Jolie said, hoping the half light hid her embarrassment. Tough girls didn't blush.

Sean didn't move. He just kept looking at her. Like a fool, she just kept looking back.

"You shouldn't look at me like that, Jo," he said finally, his voice husky. "You could get me thrown in jail."

"I'm just standing here and you're just standing there and as long as we both keep doing that, nobody's getting anything," she said, her voice sounding firmer than her knees.

Sean chuckled. "You're something else, you know that? You're not like the other chicks around here— you're smart."

Jolie liked the way Sean's eyes continued to laugh even after his mouth had moved on to something else. She cocked her head to one side, giving in for a split second to the sassy flirt she might have been if she'd lived in a safer world.

"You're right. I'm not like the other chicks you go out with; I'm younger."

Most girls would have done anything to nail a guy with a body like Sean's, but Jolie wasn't most girls.

Chapter One

She'd seen what happened to schoolgirls who got into relationships with older guys. There was no future in it. She might have a woman's body but legally she was considered a kid and he was both young enough to be irresponsible and old enough to be held accountable--a dangerous combination. Impulsive choices ruined lives. Jolie understood that even if Sean might be willing to forget.

"Guess I'll just have to wait for you to grow up, huh?"

"You're going to save yourself for me, Sean? Wow. Oops! Too late." She brushed past him. His laugh rolled over her from behind. A half dressed Rick leaned half way out of the trailer door. *Fitting*, Jolie thought. Everything about Rick was half way.

"Hey, Jo, is that Sean out there?" The dim light from inside the trailer backlit him like he was some low rent trailer park god. He would have liked that image: Rick, the warlock god of Vegas.

Rick, with his snake tattoos and slithery pets, liked to talk himself up like he was some dark-horned Keeper of the Sacred Snake and his own personal anatomical version was the altar at which every woman should worship. In Jolie's eyes, he was just a snake—no godlike mumbo jumbo about it. He didn't have any special powers or abilities no matter what he pretended. If he had, she'd have known. She knew way too much about other people's private lives, and that went triple for Rick Shanks'.

Rick would have had no trouble convincing Jessie Lynn he was endowed with special powers. When he told her he was the reincarnation of the famous, warlock Simon Magus, she would no doubt have gasped in utter belief. She'd probably kept on gasping for quite awhile.

"Sean, is that you?" Rick called out. "Hey man, you got any money? Jessie's out of brew."

"Uh, hello. Can I come in now?" Jolie crossed to the trailer's doorstep and waited for Simon Magus' reincarnation to move out of her way.

"Where've you been, Jo?" Rick grinned, undressing her with his eyes as she brushed past him. "Nice...jeans."

The tight spring inside Jolie wound a turn. *What would it be like to come home to a place where you felt safe?* "Stop looking at my butt, you perve. Where's my mom?"

"At work. They called her in early."

"I need my key back." She held out her hand.

"Sure, hon," Rick answered all wide-eyed innocence. "Your mom just wanted me to make some copies."

"A copy, Rick. A single copy and if you're going to lock the door so I can't get into my own house when I come home from school, I need my friggin' key."

"Sorry, babe, I didn't hear you. I must have been in the shower."

Jolie didn't say anything about the spare key in the tin box. Jessie and her daughter didn't have much in common these days, but they still had a few secrets: the tin box with the spare key was one of them. Jessie's old phone book buried somewhere in the bottom of one of the cardboard boxes, and the getaway money that would be stashed with it as soon as they could scrape it together again, were the others. These were the backups they always kept to themselves, no matter how close the boyfriends or other friends got. They had saved them more than once.

"Sure, babe. I'll make a copy tonight." Rick grabbed his shirt, the key, and a coat from the couch. "Sean," he shouted. "We need to make a run."

Chapter One

The two men quickly faded into the twilight.

Jolie shut and locked the trailer door. There was no telling how long Rick would be gone, a few hours, a few days maybe if she was lucky. But he had a key and as far as he and her mom were concerned; that gave him a pass. All the lock on the front door did was give Jolie a few seconds warning. It wasn't much, but it was all that stood between the scumbags her mom dated, their friends, and her. A lone female without protection was considered fair game by these modern day predators, and Jolie had no illusions about what they were capable of.

She leaned back against the trailer door, rolled her head slowly to remove the tension, and tried to wrap herself in a moment of peace. You couldn't live all wound up all the time. You had to let down your guard a little now and then.

She had told Jessie from the start that Rick was no good, but no matter how regretful her mom always was at the end of a relationship, she never listened in the beginning, or the middle, or anytime it might do any good. Only after all the shit had come down, did Jessie see the truth? Before that, she doggedly believed in every loser who slipped between her sheets. To the users and abusers, Jolie's mother attracted, a single woman who liked to party, with the added bonus of a nubile daughter, was like getting the keys to a candy store. There was just no way the goodies were going to stay in their wrappers.

Betty Boop's clock-hand legs were splayed in a Rockettes' kick indicating it was five o'clock--seven hours until Jessie got off work if she didn't take an extra shift. Chances were, she wouldn't be home until dawn. Jolie was sure that none of the preppy student council kids at school had to deal with this kind of stuff, along with all the book reports and Algebra tests, but she had stopped expecting the kind of life people said kids were supposed to have a long time ago. That didn't mean, however, that she didn't notice the differences between their lives.

Jessie Lynn Figg worked as a cocktail waitress at the Little Lucky Casino on Boulder Highway at the Southern edge of the city.

"When I get off work, I'm all wound up, babe. I can't just come home and go to sleep. I'd rattle around this box all night and keep you awake. You need your sleep so you can be smart and pass tests."

Jolie's argument that having Jessie come home at a regular hour so she didn't have to stay awake worrying would do a lot more for her grades, fell on deaf ears.

"You understand, don't you, honey?" Jessie whined.

And Jolie did. She understood that it was more important to Jessie to stay out than it was for her to come home. These days they lived in different worlds. Their problems came from the few parts that still overlapped.

Jolie looked around the tiny cluttered trailer. It was a mess. It was always a mess. It was too small to be anything else. Smells, like sounds, went right through the brown accordion doors, leaching from wherever they were supposed to be to wherever they could get and hang out there--kind of like Jessie's boyfriends.

Everything Jolie owned smelled like 'Cologne de' Hell', a combination of stale alcohol, cigarettes, toilet, mold, dirty laundry, sweaty bodies, and weed. It was a scent designed by, and for, Rick and his "buds"--sub-humans hell bent on permanent residence in the underworld. Jolie could never figure out why a guy like Sean hung out with such a bunch of losers.

The sink was full of dirty dishes, as usual. Built for the convenience of a middle-class woman with nothing to do during her husband's fishing trips except tidy up, it had the dish capacity of two cereal bowls and was a nightmare for a working mom, her daughter, and the half dozen slobs who partied there. The little dinette booth table was cluttered with empty beer bottles, fast food bags, and half empty Slurpee cups that had been used for ash trays. A stick of dollar store incense burned in a cheap dragon incense burner on the kitchen counter. It didn't help. The place reeked of pot.

Jolie weighed the drudgery of cleaning against the drudgery of doing homework. She hated both, but cleaning was a true act of futility. It didn't get you anywhere, and getting somewhere--anywhere, was something Jolie was serious about. At least homework stayed done. She didn't pretend to know much, but she knew that she didn't want to spend her life mopping someone else's dirty floors or getting her butt pinched while she served drinks to people who wouldn't remember where they'd been in the morning.

Jolie checked the lock on the trailer door one more time, then checked her phone for messages. Becca, her one friend from high school had called. Jolie slipped her phone back into her pocket. She couldn't deal with Becca right now. She made the rounds of the windows then headed to her room.

How long had it been since she'd felt safe, she wondered, fingering the leather amulet, or "hand" as Mem had called it, that hung around her neck. It was old now. She'd replaced the original leather cord twice, so now it hung by a cheap chain from the dollar store. The leather was stained with years of her sweat. Mem had instructed Jolie to "feed" it magic oil or alcohol to keep it fresh but even though she'd tried to follow her grandmother's instructions, Jolie could feel how flat the bag had become. The herbs inside were dust. The magic was worn out and Mem was not around to fix it. Her grandmother hadn't figured on Jessie Lynn bundling Jolie up in the middle of the night and leaving New Orleans, or on dying before Jolie could get back.

"We've got deep ties to this land," Mem had said. *"You may go and live in other places like your daddy did; helping people and learning other ways, but you'll always come back. This land is your heart--your anchor."* It was hard to understand how, with all her gifts of *seeing*, Mem had not foreseen that Jolie would be set adrift with no one to guide her, or renew the protection amulet that she had been given.

Jolie wasn't even sure what the bag was supposed to be protecting her from, really. She just knew that she felt better when she wore it and that the voices from other people's minds were a little kinder and not as insistent-- even now, with the magic all tired and faded. Maybe it was just the emotional connection Jolie felt to the past. Maybe there'd never been any magic about it; just a feeling that someone you loved gave something to you, believing it would keep you safe. Maybe all the bad things that had started piling up the last few years were just a coincidence and had nothing to do with the amulet losing its power. Maybe all that Mem had ever done for anyone with her healing ways, had been to convince people that someone cared.

Jolie pressed the little bag against her heart, trying to ignore the fear that rose inside her. If there really was magic in the world, even a trace of it, she desperately needed it.

CHAPTER TWO

The ground at Jolie's feet went on and on without end. There was no sky, just a black and white striped dream-eternity. Some version of Jessie Lynn was there, a zebra painted zombie staring out at the nothing while a prison-striped vampire sucked blood from her pale finger. The creature looked like Rick.

The thing looked up at Jolie as if she had called its name; its eyes striped black and white like Goth lifesavers with wide open begging mouths at their centers.

Jolie knew that the life the creature sucked from her mother was not enough. It would never be enough. The last of what he sought had run down Jessie's legs in red rivers of blood when Jolie was born.

The dream changed.

A nurse with huge blue rubber gloves was cleaning Jessie Lynn's blood from the floor. She stuffed the cloth rags, cut up pieces of a Power Rangers blanket, in a red plastic bag with "Bio Hazard" written on the side. The contaminated rags glowed through the plastic.

"Wait!" Jolie shouted, as the nurse in her crisp white uniform threw the bag, with her mother's energy in it, onto a pile of other bags just like it. It sank down, its glow fading, lost in the slush pile of toxic human waste.

Jolie jumped onto the garbage pile, clawing at the red plastic bags, desperate to find the one that held her mother's essence. None glowed. They held only dead energy. There was no way to tell one from another.

They're only the same on the outside, Jolie thought. She grabbed the nearest one and ripped it open. A terrible howl of grief and anguish rushed out at her.

Jessie Lynn screamed with pain as she labored to bring her child into the world, her screams, working like a bizarre alarm clock, calling Jolie's soul to enter the tiny physical body.

"Not yet," Jolie protested. "I have to do something. I have to find—"

"It's time, Jolie," a voice told her. It was Topi's voice; Topi who had been left behind in New Orleans.

"I'm not ready, I have to finish this first," Jolie pleaded.

"I'm sorry, darling one, but you have to come into the body now or it will die," Topi said gently.

Jolie watched the mountain of bags shrink away from her as she was sucked through a tunnel toward the squalling lump of bloody flesh entering the world. Her soul shivered, afraid of the long years it would be trapped in the little body struggling to master this new environment and mature enough to remember the wisdom of her spirit.

"How long is this for, again?" She hesitated. "How long do I have to stay?"

"It's all right. Don't be afraid. We will be with you. We'll look after you."

Cold, solid hands grabbed Jolie and pulled her from the slippery red tunnel into the empty space of physical reality. She opened her mouth and howled like a demon was chasing her.

"It's a girl, Jessie Lynn, a beautiful baby girl," the nurse said, holding the red, bawling thing up for inspection. Jolie's mother turned her face away, sobbing into her pillow.

Chapter Two

Jolie looked through physical eyes and found Topi's handsome black face bent over her.

"Welcome, Joliette Boulet," he said softly in his thick, round South African accent. "We are honored you have joined us."

Behind him were Mem, Great Aunt Jessamin, Grandpere Blancflor, and Papa Jon. There were others too, a whole crowd of them; faces of all different colors, some solid and some ghostlike-barely there, including her father's.

"Welcome," they sent her greetings. But the newborn baby did not feel welcome. She felt confused. She had been born and now she found herself inside a helpless body, unable to even move on her own. She tried to vault her spirit through the ceiling, back into the Spirit world. Nothing happened.

"What have you done to me?" She demanded. What kind of a life is this? I'm trapped. This is a trick!" All her mother and the nurse heard was a baby bawling lustily. A pair of warm arms folded around her and the world took on a rosy gold glow.

"Now then, Jolie, don't fuss so," Mem whispered, rocking the baby gently. "It will be all right by and by. It just takes some time. You'll have to re-learn a few things."

"Then let's get on with it. When do we start?" Jolie demanded.

"Patience, granddaughter, you need to adjust to physical life--grow up a bit first. Don't worry, we've got time." Jolie had just heard her first lie.

The voices and faces of the spirit people faded blocked out by the sound of her mother's sobs.

"What's wrong with her?"

"The birth was hard," Mem answered. "And she is alone. Your father is not here."

"But he was--I saw him." Jolie looked around.

"He is in the spirit world, Jolie. You will not see each other again for a long time," Mem explained.

A wave of loss swept over Jolie. It seemed so unfair. As the spirit world retreated, the physical world rushed in to replace it and Jolie felt the strong link the infant body had to the woman whose body it had shared for nine months.

"Is she all right?" She asked. "I didn't mean to hurt you. Please, don't cry."

Jessie Lynn reached out to her daughter, snagged her spirit and tied it fast to anchor it to her own. Mem's eyes looked at the young woman in alarm. Jessie glared back at her, defiantly.

"Her name is not Boulet. It's Figg and she's my child, not yours. You have no claim on her."

"She is part of our family," Mem assured Jessie. "As you are."

"The hell I am. Lucien didn't love me. He didn't care about either of us. He abandoned us."

Mem's eyes flashed. "That's unfair. He would never have done that if he'd known, and he didn't know because you didn't tell him."

Topi stepped to Jessie's side and took her hand. "Lucien is gone and whatever he did, right or wrong, cannot be changed. What we must do now is look to the living."

Mem nodded. "You have nothing to worry about Jessie. The family will look after you--you and Joliette."

Topi bent over Jessie and kissed her damp forehead. "Rest and get your strength back. We can sort all this out later."

Jessie Lynn eyed Mem suspiciously. "I am her mother," she growled.

Chapter Two

Jolie woke up on her bed in the trailer feeling like a horse had sat on her chest. She hated the birthing dream with its side dish of guilt. The feeling that she was responsible for her mother's failed existence took days to fade and then, just when she had come to grips with what she owed Jessie Lynn and what she didn't, it came again; like Jessie had put it on automatic redial with the universe.

Jolie pulled a pillow to her chest and stared at the brown water stains on the ceiling. It didn't rain in Las Vegas, but when it did, it poured through every crack in the trailer. She glanced at the clock on her dresser. It was ten minutes to seven. She was going to be late for school again.

"Shit!" She rolled out of bed. If she had to be so damned gifted, why couldn't she at least have gotten some practical talent so she could blink or wave something and everything would be fixed? But real life was not like TV.

"All of the problems and none of the perks," she muttered, slipping on jeans and patting the pocket to be sure her phone was still in there. Hunting through a short stack of clean clothes, she grabbed a tee shirt. "So much for individuality."

Jeans and a tee shirt: the school uniform of her age. Adults didn't need to dictate uniforms. All they had to do was get out of the way and let peer pressure do the job.

Jolie had seen a few variations during her gypsying around from state to state. In Colorado and Oregon they actually wore coats in the winter, something no self-respecting Californian or Southern Nevadan would ever do, no matter how cold it was. Even when the temperatures were below freezing, the fashion conscious Las Vegan wore shorts, or jeans, a tee-shirt, and maybe a hoodie--like they could change the weather by ignoring it.

Jolie scrunched her hair into knots on the sides of her head and stabbed them with hair sticks that twisted and fanned open. The straight and narrow kids, with their slicked down gelled up Barbie and Ken hair styles, might snicker, but messy was always in with the out crowd. She pulled on red Converse tennies, tying the lime green shoestrings. She didn't bother with socks. A finger-wipe of green iridescent eye shadow to draw out the violet flecks in her hazel brown eyes, a couple of strokes of mascara, a slick of lip gloss, and she was done. She grabbed a jean jacket off the hook by the door, stuffed her homework into her backpack, and removed the chain lock from her accordion door. Opening the kitchen cupboard as she flew by, she swept a granola bar into one hand, grabbing a handful of small bills off the counter with the other.

"I got my lunch money out of your tips, Mom," Jolie called out to her sleeping mother. As she headed for the door, she noted Rick's shoes tossed by the couch and remembered that Jessie was off the next two days. Rick would be staying over. She went back and stuffed most of the bills into a pocket in her backpack. With Rick there, there'd be nothing left by the time she got home from school. Whatever Jolie kept now would be all they'd have for groceries until her mom went back to work.

"Bye, Mom. Love you." She unlocked the door and slipped out into the frosty morning.

The homeless woman was sitting by the trailer park sign at the main entrance.

"What's the traffic report?" Jolie asked as she approached.

Chapter Two

"We're off to a bad start for the morning commute. Metro reports fender benders at D.I. and Boulder Highway, Rainbow Boulevard just North of the 215 and southbound on the 95 at Lake Mead..." the woman went off.

"Thanks, that'll do." Jolie pulled out a couple of small bills and put them in the old woman's hand. "Stay out of dark places and no booze."

"I don't drink," the woman said as clear as a Toastmaster graduate.

Jolie blinked. "Good."

"Thank you," the woman added, with perfect, lucidity.

"It's no big deal, but you heard what I said before about staying away from our shed, right? I don't mind if you sleep there, it's just that my mom's boyfriend is a real douche bag, and I'm not sure what he'd do if he found you, especially if he didn't think anyone would miss you." She paused. "So, would anyone miss you?"

"No." The woman's eyes glazed over and she began mumbling, "Sky View Traffic is brought to you by..."

"Well, be careful, okay?"

"You too," the woman said.

Just getting to school could be a challenge when you heard people's lives shattering around you. Jolie grimaced at the thought of sitting in detention trying to explain to Officer Cliff Wrangler why he should not write her up for truancy.

"I started to go to school, Cliff, really I did, but I passed this man on the corner who'd just found out his wife was having an affair and he was going to commit suicide and well, what was I supposed to do, just ignore him because I had an algebra test? Yes, I'm saying I didn't go to school because I was saving someone's life. No, I didn't know him but he was a fellow human being

in pain. I had to do something, right? How did I know he was going to commit suicide? The same way I knew his wife was having an affair. Would I like to explain that? No, I don't think so."

There were a lot of things about her life that Jolie couldn't explain to someone like Cliff Wrangler--things beyond the usual embarrassments of being poor and having a bar fly mom that liked to date skanky would-be warlocks. For her, there was this whole other world overlaid on the world most people saw. She couldn't explain it. She wasn't interested in even trying to. What was the point? They wouldn't believe her.

Jolie was eleven before she realized that other kids didn't see colored clouds around people or hear what their friends and their parents were thinking. After they'd left New Orleans she'd tried to talk to her mother about what she saw, but Jessie didn't really seem to pay attention. Then, Jolie told Jessie that she knew her best friend's dad was seeing someone. Jessie went into a rage, insisting that Jolie was lying.

"It's your imagination. It's made up. I don't ever want to hear you say stuff like this ever again. Do you understand?" Jessie shook Jolie by the shoulders. *"Do you understand, Jolie? Never."*

Jolie understood very well. When Jessie grabbed her, she had seen that it was her mom who was having the affair with her friend's father. The vision had not spared her the details.

It was hard to have a best friend you shared everything with, and not tell them something so important, but telling the truth had turned out to have consequences beyond Jolie's young understanding. Her friend never spoke to her again and they moved soon after.

Chapter Two

But trying to keep her talents hidden was like trying to hide a pregnancy. The more you tried, the more it hurt you, and the longer the secret went on, the messier things got. Jessie had to have noticed things, they just never mentioned it.

People say it's hard for teenager's to sort out their thoughts and feelings. They should try taking a walk in my shoes, Jolie grumped, mentally. She was tasked with sorting out her own and everybody else's feelings as well. It was like having somebody dump all their stuff in your room on top of your stuff, then trying to find something. Mem had told Jolie that their family had gifts, but that's not the way Jolie looked at it. If she could have found the receipt, she would have exchanged this gift for some good old fashioned normal in a heartbeat. Unfortunately, that store had closed and she was stuck with her white elephant. She was just going to have to find some way to learn to live with it.

CHAPTER THREE

There are two big tests in a kid's life that either make or break them as functioning human beings: family, and school. If you could survive both, you'd earned adulthood.

Everyone entering the halls of Chaparral High ran the ridicule gauntlet, no exemptions. You could put up a metal detector every ten feet and kids wouldn't feel any safer because the most hurtful attacks had nothing to do with physical weapons.

The popular kids picked at the scabs of the geeks, the preps used sledgehammers to crush the skaters, the skaters slashed at the Thezbians, the jocks staked out the Goths and the Emo's and everyone smiled at the jocks and preps while secretly fantasizing how to do them in. The unspoken code demanded that the picked on suffer in silence, their wounds unacknowledged and untreated. Most would not heal until long after the tortured tones of the school band playing Pomp and Circumstance had passed from their memories. They might not even remember who called them "zit face" or "slut," but they would remember how it made them feel, and it would mold the way they thought of themselves, and others, for the rest of their lives.

Jolie tucked her amulet under her tee shirt and patting it flat. She had enough problems at school with her bohemian thrift-store clothes, multiple piercings, and wild colored hair, she didn't need anyone asking her why she wore an old leather bag around her neck.

"Whazzup, Jo?" Rebecca fell in beside Jolie as she raced to beat the bell, her solid legs looking out of place coming out from beneath a teal and gray skort. "I tried to call you last night."

"I turned my phone off so I could focus on my homework."

Rebecca Grolund was a geek playing at being a Goth because she thought it made her cooler. She and Jolie hung out, met at the library sometimes, and once in awhile studied at Rebecca's, which was a real two-story stucco house in one of the newer developments. The problem with having friends was that you had to listen to their problems--and for, Jolie that meant what they thought as well as what they said. She found both equally lame. Rebecca didn't really have any problems. She had a two parent family that paid their bills, took family vacations, set aside money for their daughter's college, and went to parent teacher conferences. Rebecca's problems were all temporary illusions. As soon as she graduated, went to college, and realized that being smart was not an obstacle in life or something to be embarrassed about; she was going to be fine. She and Jolie had nothing in common outside of Rebecca's temporary status as an outsider, but Rebecca did have one trait that made her easier to hang out with than most; she had very little internal dialogue. She rarely had a thought that didn't just spill out of her mouth. It made being around her almost peaceful in a weird way.

"Did you hear about Megan Washburn?" Rebecca pushed her dark rimmed designer glasses back up her nose.

"No. And why would I want to."

"She broke her leg yesterday at practice." Rebecca looked at Jolie expectantly. "Did you hear me?"

"Yeah." Jolie kept walking. "She broke her leg. What was she doing, climbing off her boyfriend's face?" Jolie didn't have anything against Brad Richter personally, but anybody stupid enough to attach themselves to Megan Washburn deserved ridicule.

Rebecca rolled her eyes. "Oh come on, Jo, you don't have to pretend with me. *I know you did it,* she added silently.

Jolie's trouble meter ran straight to red alert.

"Pretend what? What are you talking about, Becca?" She was careful not to address Becca's unspoken thoughts.

"You know. *The broken leg."*

"No, I don't," Jolie said trying to keep the impatience from her voice.

"Don't you remember how yesterday you and Megan got into it, and you went off on her?"

Jolie felt like she was standing under the chute of a cement mixer, and somebody had just dumped the load.

"Yeah. I got mad, so what? She deserved it. She stole my homework and was going to copy it. If we get caught, Miss Sally Rally gets a talking to and I get probation."

"Yeah… And? *Then you did something--put a spell on her or something. I know you did."*

"And nothing," Jolie said firmly. "I told her off, and took my paper back, end of story."

"And then Megan broke her leg. *Like that was an accident? "*

"That's got nothing to do with me."

"Yeah, right. Oh, come on, Jolie. I was in your trailer. I saw all that witchy stuff; candles and skulls and stuff. You taught her a lesson, right? You did something to make Megan sorry for what she did."

"What are you, crazy? I didn't do anything."

"She's lying to me." Rebecca pressed her lips firmly together. "I don't believe you."

Chapter Three

Jolie looked Rebecca straight in the eyes. "If you were really my friend, you would. If you were my friend, Becca, you would drop this right now and never mention it again."

"She's afraid someone will find out. I'm not going to tell anyone. I won't tell a living soul. I promise, Jo."

Jolie looked at the crowded hall around them. Students streamed past in both directions. It was perfect for turning the seed of a secret into a hot house rumor.

"Plenty of dead souls around here," she said, dryly.

"You're so paranoid. Come on, I think your family being into all that witch stuff is cool."

"My mom's boyfriend is not my family, and I am not into any witch stuff," Jolie insisted.

"Whatever. It's not like they burn witches or anything anymore, you know."

Jolie did not agree. There was a cluster of girls in the hall that she knew for a fact would be happy to burn her alive, no matter what century it was, right after they shaved her head. She felt a dull throb between her shoulder blades.

"Don't be naive, Becca. There are plenty of ways to get crucified in high school, with or without a stake through your heart." Jolie could have strangled her mom for inviting Becca into their trailer. It was one of Jolie's first rules: never invite anyone over and never, ever let them inside. It had been a hard lesson. When you're young and alone and always the new kid, you want people to like you. You want to believe in things like friendship and trust, but people couldn't be trusted--even people who said they were your friends.

Rebecca puffed her black lined lips into a pout. "I still don't believe you."

"Make up whatever fantasy you want, Becca, but leave me out of it, okay?" As Jolie walked away, she noticed a girl from one of the preppie clusters, smiling like someone had paper clipped the sides of her mouth to her ears, break off and make a beeline for Rebecca. Rebecca saw the shark approaching and froze.

Sharks and Minnows: It was a game Jolie had played at the local day camp the summer they'd lived in Oregon. The sharks ran around tagging the minnows, who had to run back and forth across the field. Why? Because that was how the game was played. Once a minnow was tagged, it was frozen and had to help the sharks tag the other minnows, who only moments ago had been their teammates.

They'd played the game a lot, but none of the camp counselors had ever questioned the morality of the underlying lesson. None of the players had ever refused to turn on their former friends and remain true to their kind. Once they were tagged by the bigger faster sharks, minnows gleefully did their best to tag other minnows for their new masters, and in high school, it was every minnow for themselves.

Rebecca Grolund was a minnow among minnows. Presented with the chance to be noticed by the prettier wealthier more popular sharks, she would not be true to her minnow kind. She'd tag for the sharks, and the blood that would be spilled would be Jolie's.

Jolie ducked into English class as the bell rang, just missing getting her third tardy for the quarter. Focusing on the assignment, she barely noticed Courtney Parks come in late. Courtney gave Mrs. Winston a hall pass and headed down the aisle between the desks. Jolie felt a pinch between her shoulder blades as Courtney passed, throwing Jolie a look of pure poison. Silently, she dropped a folded note onto the desk.

Chapter Three

"Bitch, this'll get you." Jolie heard Courtney think. The note had been folded over and over until it was small enough to be easily palmed.

Pea seed origami, Jolie thought. *How bougie.* She opened the multiple folds and held the note under the edge of her desk so she could read it without being noticed by the teacher.

"What did you do?" It said in violet gel pen. Careful to show no expression, Jolie wadded the note up and stuck it in her backpack. Fifteen minutes into the period, she got a second delivery, this time by Page Del Rey.

"Please don't look up. Please don't look up," shy Page pleaded silently as she walked down the aisle. Jolie felt the eyes of the other girls on her and the uncomfortable pinch in her upper back, but there wasn't much intrigue to the game now. She knew what was coming, so she ignored the note, leaving it just sitting on her desk for awhile before casually opening it. *"Why did you do it?"* it read in round, immature script.

The third note came a few minutes later, again delivered by another cheerleader, again accompanied by the pain between her shoulders. Shalamar Johnson didn't think anything as she made her delivery, which did not surprise Jolie since Shalamar was not known for her intellect. *"We're watching you,"* this note said. Of course, they were, but Jolie was determined not to give them the satisfaction of having anything to watch.

She was taken off guard, however, when a fourth note arrived in her next class not delivered by a cheerleader. This one had only one word on it: *"witch"*.

Here we go again. Jolie groaned. Why were kids so damn mean? Didn't anybody ever stop to consider that other kids felt just as rotten when they got picked on as you did when someone picked on you? But in sharks and minnows, everyone loved tagging.

E.F. Winters

Texting in class was against the rules at Chaparral, but in the information age, there was no stopping a good piece of gossip, especially if it fit into a neat sound bite. When Jolie looked up, she could see the message sweeping through the room, kids heads diving into backpacks, hands to pockets or purses. When they emerged their eyes tracked to Jolie. All her hopes for an uneventful year vanished.

CHAPTER FOUR

Jolie avoided Rebecca at lunch, sticking to the privacy of the library. Becca didn't take choir, so Jolie could ignore the problem for fifty minutes and try to focus on the winter concert that night. She couldn't avoid History class, but Mrs. Speils was old school and they had assigned seats across the room from each other. So Jolie didn't have to face Rebecca again until the end of the day. By then, the whole school had heard how Jolie Figg had put a spell on Megan Washburn and made her break her leg.

From across the schoolyard, Jolie watched as Rebecca walked against the tide of kids toward the circle of sharks who had wooed her this morning. As soon as they spotted her, they closed ranks, turned their backs, and began to move away.

"Oooh, the cold shoulder," Jolie muttered.

Once frozen, a minnow was of little use to a shark, except to tag others of its own kind, and once they'd done what they could, they were useless. What minnows always failed to grasp, was that no matter how many of your own you tagged, it never made you a shark, and no shark was ever going to thank you for helping them.

Rebecca stopped and stared after the retreating sharks, understanding washing over her. She had been played. They had never had any interest in her. They had never intended to include or befriend her. She had simply been a means to an end, and that end had been to humiliate Jolie. Rebecca's cheeks flushed and she bit her lip. Turning away, she looked for a coral reef, a bit of seaweed--anything that could provide safety. She saw Jolie and offered a hopeful smile.

If there had been the slightest doubt in Jolie's mind where the rumor had come from, that smile would have erased it. It said it all; Rebecca had caved, spilling her imaginary truth to the carnivores. They, in turn, had accepted her offering of Jolie's friendship at their high altar of gossip, voted on Becca's unworthiness, and turned her out. Jolie looked at Becca and kept on walking. You couldn't be friends with a frozen minnow, and you sure as hell couldn't be friends with a shark, but in this game, those were the only options.

It was a long walk home alone. Jolie passed other kids walking in small groups or paired, their books hugged to their chests or sagging like rocks in their backpacks. There were loners, too, but none willing to put themselves in the shark's target zone by talking to Jolie Figg. Sometimes she felt the tell-tale sensations she got in her back when someone focused bad intentions toward her. Left to her own thoughts, Jolie's fears played and replayed different scenarios. Like that crazy woman, Scarlett O'Hara, in the old movie Gone With the Wind, Jolie kept trying to push them away, telling herself she wasn't going to think about them right now, that she'd think about it tomorrow, but she was no movie heroine and her life had not been so neatly scripted. It was a sloppy, chaotic series of train wrecks.

Jolie watched a lot of old movies when her mom was at work. Movies, especially old movies, were full of people with solvable problems. Of course, none of them resembled her problems, but secretly, she hoped that one night she'd hit the remote and there it would be; her life, torn apart, then patched back up in a neat two-hour package. With the current fad for all things magic, the odds were in her favor, but she couldn't help wondering why in the movies, people with psychic abilities all had money. Except for the brief time when Buffy had to work a fast food job, the only poverty level psychic Jolie had seen was Carrie, and that girl was just plain messed up.

As Jolie approached the entrance to the trailer park, she saw the homeless woman sitting in the same place on the brick wall where Jolie had left her that morning. She had a bucket on her head.

"What's up with the bucket?" Jolie sat down beside her.

"I'm trying to stop the waves. I think someone put little radios in my teeth," the woman whispered conspiratorially. "I hear them. Drives me crazy."

"Ah." Jolie wasn't sure how to follow this line of conversation without it getting weird and judgmental. "So, you've just been sitting here all day?" she changed the subject.

"Don't have any place to go. This seems as good as anywhere."

"It's not. There are better places, there have to be. My grandmother always said this was an amazing world. I don't know where the amazing parts are, but they sure as hell aren't in this dump."

"Bad day?" the old woman asked.

"It's high school." Jolie shrugged. "What can I say? So where's your blanket?"

A little smile turned up the corners of the woman's thin lips. "Did you know that the little boy in twenty-four B's favorite thing in the whole world is the Power Rangers? He's a sweet kid. You don't mind, do you?"

Jolie shook her head. "I'm pretty much over the Power Ranger stage. Anyway, we got a box in our shed that just spits out old blankets, one after the other. So help yourself. Just make sure Rick's not around."

The old woman's eyes glazed over. "On I-fifteen Northbound we've got the usual slow down as you approach Flamingo, all the way up to Sahara...." It was news time.

Jolie walked slowly through the trailer park as the sun edged toward the west hills. Trailers: a bunch of metal boxes with all the conveniences of home and none of the commitments. You could put on nice clothes, drive away and pretend you were just like everybody else, but sooner or later, you had to come home, and then everything turned back into pumpkin shells and rats.

No one lived at the Paradise Trailer Haven because they wanted to. Some choice in their lives had dumped them here. Nobody ever said, "When I grow up I want to live in a trailer park, in the low-rent part of town, so my kids can go to overcrowded underfunded schools, and get laughed at when they wear the wrong kinds of clothes and have holes in their shoes," but somehow it happened, and families still managed to stick together… or not.

In a trailer park you couldn't hide anything. Everybody knew everybody else's business. Walls were thin so you heard everything that went on. There's just no privacy in a world where people can hear you flush after your morning dump.

Unless people argued in whispers, which they did not, your neighbors were going to hear all the gritty details of your life. They were going to take sides and they were going to keep score. In the summer, when everyone was outside because of the heat, money would change hands. The cheap thrills of Reality TV had its roots in trailer life.

Residents handled this lack of privacy in two ways: they joined the community, acknowledging their common link, giving and getting advice from their

Chapter Four

fellow down-and-outers, or they spit at the world, pulled into themselves and went all Howard Hughes. Rich people talked about needing to return to the village; trailer folk had never left. They'd just traded tee-pees or grass huts for metal boxes, and kept right on living hand to mouth. It might not even have been such a bad place to live if it weren't for predators like Rick. Even outside high school, there were sharks and minnows.

Jolie hesitated as she neared their trailer. Rick's El Camino was parked out front. The sun dipped down below the horizon. It was Wednesday, the night of the school's winter concert, and ignorant of his faux pas, the choir teacher, Mr. Nelson, had given the new girl a solo. Jolie was still thinking about whether to show up or not. She could be sick. No one could prove she wasn't. There were lots of bugs going around. But the concert was a big part of her grade and as dorky as it would probably be, with its cheap red punch and cardboard cookies, she needed to go.

Something about the size of a cat slunk around under the trailer. Jolie's fingers reached for her amulet. Dark and skinny, it was like a runny ink blot in the air. A tingling fear played on the small keys of her upper spine; a tiny warning bell ringing in the darkness. Jolie had even thought it was a cat the first time she saw it, but it didn't really move like a cat. It moved like something trapped on the evolutionary ladder between an ape and a man, and it hung out around Rick; something he'd picked up with some of the other garbage he collected.

Jolie shivered. She could feel its energy from where she stood. It felt icky and wrong.

The trailer was dark, except for a red glow coming from the dinette area. Shadows moved beyond the drawn curtains. Rick and Jessie Lynn were spell casting. Jolie didn't need to see it, she could feel it; the elemental powers that had been called to witness, the small spirits and demons summoned to heel, waiting on the spell caster's will: Rick's will. It was bad stuff, like him. Jolie didn't know what Rick thought he was doing. He couldn't control the things he called. He didn't even take responsibility for having called them. He just left them to wander around, and they did, usually close to wherever he'd called them, which unfortunately meant her trailer.

"Shit," Jolie muttered. The energy left behind after one of these sessions coated everything with a heavy film that felt like a layer of congealed grease, making everything nearby dull and lifeless. She had no idea how to get rid of it. What she did know was that she didn't want to be anywhere near it. She thought about going to the library, or Jack In The Box, or just going back to school and waiting until Mr. Nelson opened the music room. Other kids would arrive for the concert freshly showered and groomed. They would have had nice, if slightly rushed, dinners, and be wearing new holiday sweaters or dresses under their robes--even though no one would see them except for the few minutes they spent having cheap cookies and punch. Hopefully, no one would notice that Jolie was still wearing the same jeans and tee shirt she had worn to school that day, but going to the trailer right now to change, was not an option. Jolie turned around and headed back out of the trailer park.

Going to the Winter Concert by herself was no big deal. She'd gone to dozens of school events alone. This time at least, she would know where her mom was and why she wasn't there. It might even be a good thing in light of the message-quake going on at school. If someone said something mean, who knew what Jessie would say back? If Jessie didn't come, she wouldn't be

Chapter Four

able to embarrass her daughter, Jolie tried to look on the bright side.

By nine o'clock the concert was over. Jolie avoided the punch and cookies line with its small-talking parents and headed straight for the storage room where the robes were kept. Slipping out of hers, she quickly hung it up on the rack and made a bee-line for the side door. Five minutes after the last note had faded, she was outside patting herself on the back for having gotten through the concert without incident, but the wind had kicked up, and the temperature had dropped. She was going to be a popsicle by the time she got home. A few blocks later, the warmth of the trailer sounded pretty good. Jolie hurried toward the street that led into the park.

The lights in the trailer were all on now. Metallica blared from the CD player, but Rick's car wasn't there. Jolie's hopes rose.

They fell as soon as she opened the door.

"There she is," Rick greeted her with his infuriating smile. "Where've you been, hon? Your mom and I've been worried about you."

"Hi, Mom." Jolie took note of the leftover traces of a ceremony, a pile of burnt ashes in an ashtray, Rick's ritual dagger, and an odd looking rock left on the table beside the beer and potato chips. *Sloppy.* Mem had always been very particular about separating sacred things from worldly things. Rick wasn't. Jolie examined her mother. Jessie Lynn looked like she'd worked a twelve-hour shift at the bar; anger and frustration hovering around her like a storm cloud.

"You missed the concert," Jolie said, ignoring Rick.

Jessie Lynn's reaction was no reaction.

"My school concert, Mom... Remember, I told you last week that it was tonight?" Jolie had learned early that if her mom was in a bad mood, her best defense was to redirect Jessie's focus on her deficiencies as a parent. It wasn't hard. Her mom gave her plenty to work with. "You said you'd come if you weren't working."

"I did? I'm sorry, Jo."

"Whatever. Don't worry about it. It's no big deal. I had a solo, but you know, it was just a dumb school thing. It pretty much sucked." She let her mom off the hook as she opened a Burger King sack on the counter and fished out a few stale fries from the bottom. "Was this dinner?" She moved casually from subject to subject like they were having a normal conversation. They weren't. Jessie wasn't holding up her half, she was just too drunk to realize it.

Jolie had felt kind of bad the first time she'd played the guilt card to keep her mom from fighting, but the next time she'd seen the storm clouds and let things run their natural course, she'd gotten a busted lip and grounded for a month--like she went anywhere anyway. But it was the injustice that bugged her. It was this whole "where have you been you little bitch" scenario that her mom got into that Jolie resented most as if Jessie really cared about where her daughter was beyond her own selfish desire not to have to wonder. Of course, it was okay for Jolie to have to worry about where Jessie was, that was different.

"Well, I've got to get up early, so I'm gonna hit the hay. G'night." Jolie kissed her mom on the cheek. "Night, Rick." She had almost made it to her room when Rick spoke up.

"Where's mine? Don't I get a kiss?"

Jolie felt a stab in her upper back. "Sorry, I'm all out."

He was across the room in two seconds, a hairy arm blocking the door to Jolie's room so that she couldn't

Chapter Four

pull the door closed. Jolie's heart was running the Kentucky Derby.

"Just wait a minute there, girlie. So, me and your mom are going to this thing on Friday night for Solstice and we want you to come."

Jolie tried to control her breathing, hoping that what he was saying was really all the conversation was going to be about. The Solstice gatherings at Mem's had been a big deal; sultry jazz floating over long tables heaped with food, the heady mix of it all embracing you like a pair of big soft arms. Jolie wondered what a Solstice celebration in Las Vegas would be like. If Rick was involved, she wasn't sure she wanted to find out.

"What kind of a thing?" she asked, cautiously.

"A ceremony with the coven ladies from Boulder City."

Coven ladies; Jolie got a sick feeling in her stomach. "I'm pretty busy at school...."

"School's out on Friday," Rick pointed out.

"Yeah, but we'll be loaded up with projects over the break, and I was talking to the manager at Jack In The Box about working there during vacation...."

"You've been asked special, Jolie," Jessie Lynn broke in. "It's an honor. They need you, honey. Come on. It would make Mem so proud."

Jolie glared at her mother at the mention of Mem. How dare Jessie mention her grandmother as if she cared about her?

"And we haven't done anything special for Solstice for years. I bet you miss it."

That was true.

"This is the most ancient holiday," Mem used to say. *"The real thing, made by the stars, not by men."*

"What do they need me for?"

"They need a virgin." Rick leered. "You are still a virgin, aren't you, Jo?"

Jolie ignored the question. "Why do they need a virgin?"

"What does anybody need with a virgin?" Rick began dancing around thrusting his pelvis back and forth. He seemed to have gotten all his ideas about witchcraft from bad horror films. His ceremonies had nothing to do with honoring the earth, or any of the things Mem had taught Jolie. They were about blood, skulls, power, and sex. Jolie looked to her mom for some kind of support but Jessie Lynn was only semi-conscious. What had her father, Lucien Boulet, ever seen in someone like Jessie Lynn Figg?

"Answer the question," Rick pressed. "And don't lie. A lot of people would be counting on you and I'll know if you do. I can tell when people are lying to me. I can see it like a snake sees fear in its prey."

Jolie's mind raced through the two most likely scenarios for either answer. Neither was good, but lying and answering no, was more likely to get her slapped right now than telling the truth. Whatever it was they wanted her to do, was days off. Anything could happen in a few days.

"Yes," she answered honestly. "I am."

"Sweet." Rick licked his lips, facing away from Jessie so she wouldn't see.

"Look, I told you, I'm going to get a job. I'll be too busy."

"If the guy hires you, you tell him you can start on Sunday. You should spend some time with your mom on the holidays," Rick insisted. "It'll be a family thing."

Jolie looked over at her mom. Nothing. Jolie was on her own.

Chapter Four

"Sure. Fine, if that's what Mom wants." She closed the door. Maybe they'd forget between now and then, or maybe by Friday she just wouldn't be a virgin anymore. She was pretty sure that wouldn't be too hard to arrange.

CHAPTER FIVE

Jolie cut through the casino parking lot headed for school, passing a leftover drunk and casino workers going home after the early shift. Tomorrow was here and she had no plan. She started going over her options, then decided she'd have to wait and let the sharks make the first move. A text came in. It was from Becca. *"I'm sorry"*, it read. Jolie erased it and stuck the phone back in her pocket.

The day started out uneventful. She ignored the whispers in the halls and classrooms, but she heard them, and she could feel their looks as if they were burning holes in her back.

Things came to a head at lunch when Jolie made the strategic error of thinking she could slip in under the radar and get something to eat. She realized her mistake the moment she felt the sharp stabbing pain between her shoulders. Deciding maybe she wasn't all that hungry after all, Jolie began to retrace her steps when Lindsey Johnson and her trio of minions surrounded her, bumping her into Hugo Matias, knocking his lunch tray over them both.

"How can you live with yourself?" Lindsey sneered, looking disdainfully at Jolie's soiled clothes. "Did you really think we wouldn't find out it was you, witch?"

"What'd she say?" Hugo asked, mesmerized by the foursome's hips swinging in unison, in their little bun warmer skirts, as they walked away.

"Nothing," Jolie lied. "She just called me a bitch. Whatever, you know?"

Chapter Five

"Yeah, right, whatever." Hugo shook his head, breaking the spell of the harmonic moment. Someone like Hugo wasn't even supposed to look at girls like Lindsey. No one worried about dating outside their religion, race, or culture anymore, but the social status hierarchy based on a person's coolness factor was as strong as ever. Hugo looked down at his Boba Fett shirt. The tomato sauce blended in with the mottled olive green and brown blotches.

"It's not like I really needed seconds." Hugo was a big boy with a big brain and a small life.

Don't worry. High school's not forever, Jolie wanted to tell him, but she didn't say anything. Hugo would have been mortified if she'd broken the code and openly acknowledged that either of them was being targeted for humiliation by the in-crowd.

"Yeah, well in ten years you'll be traveling the world for Google while they're getting nipped and tucked, trying to keep their misogynist car salesman husbands from screwing their bookkeepers."

Hugo grinned. "Right."

In spite of the code against speaking out about the tortures meted out by the social kings and queens of Chaparral, not all of its staff was blind and dumb, so Jolie was not surprised when she was called out of fifth period to go to the counselor's office. She knew the drill. She'd been here before; different school, different names; same scenario.

"Jolie, please come in." Ms. Warren, the school counselor, wore her curly brown hair pulled back in a severe ponytail bunched at the nape of her neck. Petite earrings, wire-rimmed glasses, and a stylish suit coat made it clear to anyone who missed the framed diploma on the wall that Ms. Warren was a Mensa candidate.

Jolie didn't know much about psychology types except that they loved to talk, so that's what she planned on letting Ms. Warren do; talk--on any subject the woman wanted to talk about: art, politics, the state of the world, herself...everything except Jolie's problems. School counselors always said they were there for you, but what that meant in practice was, they talked until they convinced themselves that you felt better. And how did they know that you felt better? Well, because they felt better and once that happened, they felt okay sending you back to class, reassured that you were patched up now, and all was right with your world.

"How are things going?" Ms. Warren asked with an overly cheerful smile. "*She looks like a tough cookie*," Jolie heard the woman think.

"Fine," Jolie answered. She didn't really do chatty. Coming in all fake smiles and spilling some made up story might work on an old school bleeding heart, but a smart thing like Ms. Warren would recognize that as unnatural behavior.

"Are you making new friends here at Chaparral?" Ms. Warren asked. *"Looking like that, probably not."*

"A few," Jolie lied.

"What about your teachers? Do you get along okay with your teachers? *I haven't seen her in here before this, so she must be doing okay with her academics*," Ms. Warren thought as she flipped through Jolie's file.

"I guess."

"Good. So, Jolie, is there anything special going on that you'd like to talk to me about?"

"You called me in, Ms. Warren."

"So I did. I thought maybe, with you being new and all, that you might need to talk to someone?"

"No. Not really, but thanks." She waited. Nothing happened. "Can I go back to class now? We're reviewing for the semester tests."

"In a minute." The woman set the file aside." *Cliff warned me she was smart."*

Cliff Wrangler, the Probation Officer. Jolie realized he and Ms. Warren have been talking about me. *Great. That just makes everything perfect.*

Jolie hadn't been here a month before she'd gotten on Cliff Wrangler's radar. Her mom and Rick had a drunken row and somebody had called the cops, but by the time they showed up, Rick and Jessie had gone off to some party where, presumably, the hosts hadn't run out of booze. After talking to the officer awhile he'd left, only to be replaced by a visit from Cliff Wrangler, Probation Officer for Clark County. She hadn't done anything wrong yet; just being her mother's daughter wasn't illegal, but it was clear from his attitude that he expected her to run amok at any moment. If he was a betting man, he'd have bet on it.

"What about these rumors going around school?" Ms. Warren asked. "That doesn't bother you? *The ones about you casting spells on people? "*

"I don't really listen to rumors, Ms. Warren," Jolie answered carefully. "I'm not here for the social life. I'm here to get a diploma."

"That's great. That's what school's for, isn't it? It's a good goal. *Wow, that was stupid. Let's try this another way.* Jolie, what do you know about witchcraft?"

Jolie got very quiet inside. The conversation suddenly felt like a cat and mouse game.

"Just what any kid knows, what I see in the movies and on TV."

"And what you read in books? Surely you read all the popular books?" Ms. Warren asked silently.

Jolie did not add anything to her list; certainly not books.

"So, do you know what a coven is?"

"Sure, it's a kind of club for witches."

Ms. Warren raised an eyebrow. "Have you ever been to a coven meeting?"

"Oh yeah, lots of times," Jolie disguised the truth with sarcasm.

"Stay straightforward and honest," Ms. Warren coached herself. "Have you ever cast a spell?"

"You're kidding, right? Of course not."

"Never?"

"I think I'd remember if I had, especially if it worked, which, of course, it wouldn't because there is no such thing as magic except in fiction or the movies."

"Did you ever tell anyone that you had cast a spell, maybe to scare them or impress them? *Like Courtney Parks or Paige Del Rey?"*

"No. I don't even know those girls." Jolie froze, waiting to see if Ms. Warren would notice her slip. "Why would I do something dumb like that?" she added quickly.

"You never told anyone that you were a witch? *Don't lie now."*

"No, because I'm not."

"She must have said something to someone. So, where'd the idea come from?"

"I think you'd have to ask the person who started the rumor."

"Do you know who that is?"

Jolie considered breaking the code. She could name a shark, one of the early girls in the campaign against her, and maybe get them in trouble for all of two seconds, hardly worth the effort or she could name Rebecca, not entirely unfair or untrue, but not Jolie's style. Rebecca had been stupid, but she wasn't a bad person. She was a minnow and she didn't deserve being hunted like a shark.

"No," Jolie answered finally. "I don't." Technically it wasn't a lie.

"Hmmm", Ms. Warren thought for a moment. *"Why don't I believe her?* Witchcraft is not a game, you know, Jolie. There are people who are very serious about it. I'm not saying I believe their claims, but the fact that they do makes them very dangerous."

Jolie didn't say anything. Ms. Warren didn't either. The game had changed to chicken now. When it was clear that Jolie would not break, the counselor finally gave in. "You're not going to tell me anything, are you?"

"There's really nothing for me to say. I haven't done anything. I'm not a witch. I never said I was a witch, and I'm not trying to become one. I'm just the new kid. You know how it is; you probably see it every year. It's always open season on the new kid, right? I figure if I don't make a big deal about this it'll blow over by the end of the break." *And everyone will just ignore me again.*

Ms. Warren studied Jolie's face then wrote something on a piece of paper and held it out to her.

"This is the address and phone number of a friend of mine who's a sort of expert on the paranormal, witches, and the occult. Just in case you decide you need someone to talk to. Okay?"

Jolie wondered what sort of an expert was. If it was like being sort of pregnant or sort of drunk, she didn't have much faith in any advice this friend could offer.

"I can't see any reason I would need it." She made no move to take the paper.

"But you'll take it to be polite and humor me, right?"

"Sure." Jolie took the paper and stashed it in a pocket of her backpack. "So, can I go now?"

"Of course." Ms. Warren nodded, moving Jolie's file to the side. *"I'll have to call Cliff and let him know what's going on."*

Don't! Jolie shouted at the counselor silently. She thought fast, "Look, my mom and I have had some trouble at home lately with one of her boyfriends and it's kind of put me on Juvenile Probation's radar. This isn't going to go on my record or anything, right?" Jolie bit her lip for good effect.

Ms. Warren reassessed her decision to call Cliff Wrangler. "No. No need for that. You haven't done anything wrong."

"Right. I haven't. Thanks, Ms. Warren." Jolie added a tentative smile--nothing over the top, just a tiny bit of a thing that showed how out of practice she was at it.

When the last bell of the day rang, Jolie headed for her locker. There was only one more day before Winter Break. If she could make it through tomorrow, time would work in her favor. After two weeks of drama-filled vacation--the hook ups and break ups, acquisitions and betrayals of teens in angst, the oddities of Jolie Figg would be old news.

Two girls giggled, whispering as they passed Jolie in the hall, then burst into laughter. A phalanx of moody Goths followed by a group of Skaters stared, their blood-colored lips pursed, hair spiked like stars radiating from their heads.

As Jolie got closer to her locker, the traffic got thicker, and her back began to hurt. A crowd had gathered in the corridor.

"What's she got in there, an oven?" someone joked.

"Watch out, she'll feed you some brownies and stick your face in her oven."

Chapter Five

"Man, it stinks!"

"Witches brew."

"Maybe it's love potion number nine!"

Those closest to her saw Jolie and suddenly the crowd parted like hair on its way to pigtails.

The word "witch" had been scrawled across Jolie's locker door. Purple smoke was streaming out around the door's edges and spewing from the vent holes.

Everyone waited to see what Jolie would do--even Jolie. She squared her shoulders and walked defiantly forward.

"Wow, you guys, and here I thought I hadn't made any friends." Holding her breath, she twirled through her combination. The door opened and a cherry bomb rolled out. "Let's play soccer." Jolie swung her leg back and gave it a good kick. "Bombs away!" The girls screamed. The boys laughed. Everyone scattered. The cherry bomb skimmed along the floor, trailing smoke and stink. It flew off the upper floor and disappeared down the stairwell. Screeches rose from below as it fell onto each lower floor. The crowd dispersed, running downstairs, following the action.

Jolie tossed out the charred mess that was everything that had been in the bottom of her locker, careful not to burn her fingers. They came away black with soot. She took a half melted lipstick from the wire tray attached to the inside of the door, closed the door and examined the message.

"Man, kids in this school really can't spell." She crossed out the "w" and made a "b" in red lipstick. A few of the kids who were still hanging around their own lockers chuckled, others just moved on. The show was over, and there were no entrails to be picked over. Suddenly, Rebecca appeared at Jolie's elbow.

"I am so sorry, Jo."

Jolie shrugged her shoulders. "Whatever. It's survival of the fittest, right?"

"Wow. You're amazing. Nothing gets to you, does it?"

Jolie whipped around. "What did you expect me to do, Rebecca? Cry? Go running to the principle, or maybe you thought I'd spill my guts to Ms. Warren?"

The look on Rebecca's face told Jolie her suspicions had been right, Becca had told Ms. Warren. She probably thought she was being a good friend, making up for her mistake. Rebecca did not understand grownups the way Jolie did. Tears glittered in Jolie's eyes, but they would not fall. She pressed her lips together and blinked them back. "Tell me, what else I could have done and still show my face around this school?"

Rebecca hung her head. "I don't know what to say, Jo." Her own eyes welled with tears. "*I blew it. She was my only friend and I totally threw her in front of the bus. I'm such a loser.*"

"Forget it," Jolie said. "It's just kid stuff, right? No big deal." Rebecca wasn't mean hearted. She'd just been used by those who played the game better than she did.

Becca's face brightened. "So, I'll see you tomorrow?"

"I'll be here."

Outside, Jolie eyed the terrain from the top of the steps before she moved, like a general sussing out a battlefield. The buses had left and most of the students were gone--enough so that those still hanging around stood out, especially the cluster of boys lounging around Brad Richter's shiny new red pickup. Brad and Megan were the Barbie and Ken of Chaparral High.

Chapter Five

What I wouldn't give for a bucketful of horse shit right now, Jolie thought. *I know just where I'd put it- splat.*

A fat pigeon vaulted across the hood of Brad's truck and let fly.

Everyone, except Brad and Jolie, cracked up. Brad's eyes found her on the steps and scowled at her like it was her fault, his body visibly gathering the courage to confront her with the accusation. The sharp stab between her shoulder blades was so powerful that it made her gasp.

"Come on you coward. I dare you," Jolie said through gritted teeth. "You and your friends only outweigh me by a couple of hundred thousand pounds."

Beep-Beep. A motorcycle horn honked from the street as Sean Flahretty pulled up.

"Hey, Jo! Come on. I'll give you a lift." Wearing tight jeans, a gray sweater, a black leather jacket and dark sunglasses, he looked every inch a teenage girls fantasy. She'd never been so happy to see the hunk in her life. Racing down the steps, she sprinted across the school lawn and vaulted onto the back of Sean's bike. Leaning forward she planted a big kiss on his cheek.

"Wow, what's that for?"

"Saving my life." She wrapped her arms around his middle.

"Gee, and I thought I was just picking you up from school."

"That shows what you remember about high school."

"Oh, I remember," he said dryly.

"Yeah? Well, it's changed since your day. Duck and cover isn't about hiding from Russian attacks anymore. It's the kids that have gone nuclear."

"Duck and cover? Just how old do you think I am, you young whippersnapper?" Sean took in Brad and his gang. "And I don't know, but it looks pretty much the same to me. There's still a bunch of punks pushing their weight around trying to make themselves look more important than they are."

"And ending up just looking stupid," Jolie added. "Come on, let's get out of here."

"Your wish is my command, Mi'Lady." Sean revved up his Harley.

Two dozen sets of envious eyes followed them. Whatever had been Tweeted, Facebooked, or splashed across her locker, every girl in sight right now, wished she was Jolie Figg, and that suited Jolie just fine.

CHAPTER SIX

"**W**here are we going?" Jolie shouted over the purr of the motorcycle's engine as Sean turned onto Boulder Highway and away from the trailer park.

"Boulder City. There's some people there who want to meet you."

Jolie's stomach got tight. "What people?"

"The coven ladies." Jolie wasn't sure she wanted to do that. As if sensing her hesitation Sean added, "Don't worry, you'll like them. Trust me."

Jolie hated it when people said that: trust me, like some slippery used car salesman. But she had escaped the snarky sharks at school, the sun was shining, and riding with the wind in her face, and her arms around Sean's taut middle, felt as good as anything in a long time. So she stayed and held on.

Boulder City was a small suburban enclave of artsy-fartsy and metaphysical types with enough yuppies thrown in to keep the place running. It had been founded as a town without gambling or alcohol in an attempt to keep the workers hired to build Hoover Dam on the job and away from the temptations of fast living. The ban on alcohol had been lifted in 1969, but gambling remained taboo. If you wanted to gamble, you had to go over the hill to Henderson or Las Vegas.

The business route that cut through downtown Boulder was still an old-fashioned two-lane affair. A modern, wider bypass built in the eighties had left the old main street looking like a throwback to the nineteen fifties, with a soda shop, little mom and pop stores, and an old theater restored by Desi Arnaz Jr: the Little Ricky of I Love Lucy fame. The marquee above the theater's entrance read "Boulder Ballet presents Babes in Toyland" and as Jolie and Sean approached, little girls in pastel tutus were pirouetting and pleiing out of SUV's under the Spanish arches and through the glass doors, flitting like butterflies into the lights. Jolie watched the delicate ballerinas disappear into the theater. It was the luck of the draw; some kids got Babes in Toyland and some got Night of the Damned. Government and social service organizations spent hundreds of thousands of dollars trying to figure out why, but no one had discovered the definitive secret to balancing this childhood injustice.

The Harley zoomed past the theater, cracking the picturesque scene's thin veneer. The wind blew a tear across Jolie's cheek, and she pressed it against Sean's back, snuggling into the warm scent of his leather jacket. It was stupid to cry over something you'd never had. She was a loner, she reminded herself. She didn't need people. It was a convenient tough-girl sort of lie, but the truth was, she felt alone and exposed all the time--except now. She closed her eyes, imagining that she and Sean could ride on forever; just the two of them, and somehow, magically, the rest of the world would not follow.

Sean turned down a side street. The bare branches of large oak trees along either side almost touched in the middle of the street. Jolie looked up at the bright blue winter sky, then turned back to watch the neat sidewalk defined yards and old bungalow style houses passing by. Sean slowed, turned the bike into a driveway, and shut it down.

"This is it." He waited for Jolie to slide off the back, then set the kickstand and swung his leg over. "Come on in."

Chapter Six

Jolie hesitated.

"They don't bite. They're domesticated witches." He took her hand and gently pulled her toward the door.

Jolie's hand felt small wrapped inside Sean's and she thought how easy it would be to just let go of her own life, and follow him wherever he wanted her to go.

She wriggled her hand from his grasp and stuck it firmly in her pocket. Sean looked back, the surprise and hurt he felt at this simple withdrawal, clear on his face.

"We wouldn't want to give them the wrong impression," Jolie explained, wishing she could take it back the moment she said it.

"Right." Sean nodded; his lips tight.

A classic front porch with square pillars gave the house an old-fashioned welcoming look, while large trees cast bare-branch shadows over the front lawn and the cement walkway leading to the front steps. The white siding and shake roof seemed out of place in this land of stucco and red tile roofs, reminding Jolie more of houses she'd seen in Oregon and Northern California. Overgrown bushes, their upper branches reaching the height of the roof, crowded the walkway leading to the back of the house.

"Whose place is this?" Jolie asked.

"My aunt's. She and my grandmother live here together." Sean led her up to the front door. An evergreen wreath with a star in the middle gave a holiday welcome. Holly and ivy crowned the upper door sill. "Aunt Mae, we're here," Sean called out as they entered.

Inside, the house was pretentious in a fussy school-teacher sort of way, but it felt clean, physically and energetically. A small group of women were gathered in the living room, seated in overstuffed chairs or on large pillows on the floor. They stopped talking as Jolie and Sean entered.

"Sean dear, it's nice to see you," an older woman, with white hair brushed into waves around her face, stepped forward to kiss Sean on the cheek. There was not a crease to be seen on her tailored navy blue dress with its white lace collar. She examined Jolie with a critical eye.

"Clearly the Figg woman's get." Jolie was judged and found lacking by association.

"I'm Sean's Aunt, Mae." She offered her hand in a gesture that was polite but held no welcome.

"And this is Jolie," Sean announced, unaware of his aunt's disapproval.

Jolie felt the eyes of the other ladies on her.

"We've met your mother. *I'm going to kill that boy*," Mae thought. Jolie's shoulder blades itched.

"Me too," She quipped, unable to restrain herself.

The four women in the living room were as different from each other as possible. One had white hair, like Mae's, but where Mae was large boned, tall, and imposing, this woman was a petite fashion plate straight from the pages of Vogue. Dressed in pleated trousers and a cardigan, she wore large gold hoop earrings, a bracelet, and a natty red tam o' shanter that matched her bright red lipstick.

"This is Iris." Mae introduced her. Iris nodded. "This is Claire." The plain woman looked at Jolie without smiling. Jolie found it hard to place Claire's age. She could have been a middle-aged woman who looked older or an older woman who looked middle-aged. The plaid wool skirt and baggy sweater she wore offered no clue. It would have been equally out of fashion anytime in the last forty years.

Chapter Six

The third woman was younger. She wore jeans, a sweater, and no make-up. Her hair was pulled back in a quick ponytail, as if she'd tried to quickly get it out of the way, like shoving your undies in a drawer before company comes. Dark brown curls had escaped the hair band, though, giving her the worn look of an angelic housewife.

"And this is Mickey."

"Hello, Jolie," Mickey responded with a little self-conscious wave.

"Hi." Jolie liked her immediately.

"And this..." Sean led Jolie into an adjoining sitting room, "is my grandmother, Faith McBride."

"She's napping, Sean. Leave her be," Iris cautioned.

"I'm not. I'm just resting my eyes," Faith countered.

"Yeah, Grandma's too contrary to actually sleep." Sean's eyes crinkled as he smiled with affection.

"Who raised this boy, Mae? He's got no manners at all, talking about his elders like when they aren't even in the room. If your Uncle Robert was still alive, I'd send you out to the shed with a switch, young man."

"Yeah, and we'd probably use it to go fishing. Uncle Robert had too much of Grandpa in him to whip anybody. He wasn't mean like you."

Faith chuckled. "Mae, go visit with the ladies, and Sean, go get yourself something to eat while I have a chat with this young lady." Mae went reluctantly; Sean, less so.

Faith shook her head and sighed. "Fast boys, what can we do? Loving them doesn't keep them out of trouble." She turned to Jolie. Her eyes were so blue it was like someone had pasted patches of the sky onto her face. Though her eyelids were as thin and fragile as dragonfly wings, the eyes beneath them snapped with wit and intelligence.

She must be an angel, Jolie thought.

Faith chuckled again. "Not yet."

Jolie looked confused. Did Faith say something? Had she heard her?

Faith raised her voice to speak to the women in the other room. "You girls stop eavesdropping and mind your own business. Jolie and I need to talk private." The chatter in the next room rose, giving them some privacy. "Come sit by me and let me have a look at you."

Jolie's heartbeat picked up. She wasn't sure she wanted to do that. What would this woman see in her? She had read plenty of people's minds, but she'd never met anyone outside her family who could read hers.

"You heard my thoughts just now, didn't you? You're gifted," she whispered.

"Mostly just old." Faith dismissed her gifts then gestured for Jolie to move closer. "Old people hear things all the time as they get closer to the other world. It's quite natural really. In other cultures, it's recognized, and they are treasured for their wisdom because of it."

"The doctors told my grandmother, Mem, that she was getting senile."

"What's real for some of us, is hard to accept for others."

"But you heard my thoughts just now. That seems pretty real to me."

Faith's laughter sounded like the bubbles in warm pudding. "Thoughts don't have that much reality. They're just stories we tell ourselves to give life form so it doesn't seem so frightening."

Jolie picked up a nearby chair and moved it over beside Faith's. As she leaned over, her amulet slipped out from under her shirt, swinging freely in the space between them. Jolie's and Faith's eyes met as Jolie quickly tucked the bag back out of sight.

Chapter Six

"That's worn out," Faith said, quietly. "The magic is tired." Jolie didn't speak. "Interesting. Sean didn't tell me you were special." Jolie just stared at her, afraid to speak. "He doesn't know, does he?" Jolie shook her head slowly. "And your mother and Rick?" Faith said Rick's name like it left a bad taste in her mouth.

"Mom must know, but she doesn't like me to talk about it. It's easier that way."

"For who? Maybe for her, but what about you?"

"I do okay."

"You've never confided in Rick?"

Jolie rolled her eyes. "Oh god, no."

"That's good. Still, someone knew." Faith's eyes looked at the bulge under Jolie's shirt. Jolie's hand clutched the amulet protectively.

"My grandmother, Mem; Lucy Boulet," Jolie explained.

"New Orleans? You're a long way from home Miss Boulet."

"Figg," Jolie corrected her.

Faith frowned. "Figg, what's that?"

"Our name: mine and my mom's, my father was Lucien Boulet, but he died before I was born."

"I'm sorry."

Jolie shrugged. "I never knew him. They weren't married and it was a long time ago."

"Well, your mother can call you a Figg all she wants, but it won't hide who you really are; you're a Boulet. You have their bloodline and their gifts. That's why your grandmother gave you that." Faith pointed to the leather bag.

"You seem to know a lot about my family and this magic stuff."

"Hardly anything."

"I've tried to take care of it like Mem told me." Jolie fondled the bag. "But it's been too long. I can feel it losing its charm or whatever it is. It's weaker now." She looked hopefully at Faith. "Can you fix it?"

Faith shook her head. "Root Magic is not my way. If you want it renewed, you should go back to the Boulet's. They'll know what's to be done."

"I don't know... Maybe, when I graduate in a few years...."

"No. It must be sooner," Faith cautioned. "It's important to protect the young, especially the gifted. This is a very powerful time for you, Jolie."

"I don't know, other people don't go around with little bags of weird stuff hanging around their necks, and they seem to do okay."

"A Boulet with gifts is not other people, and how do you know they don't have their own amulets? Maybe they're just hiding them under their shirts as well. Have you ever seen anyone wearing a cross, a special tattoo or prayer beads?"

"Sure."

"All just different kinds of amulets." Mae came around the corner, walking toward them and instantly Faith's manner changed. "So what about it, Jolie, will you be our Solstice Maiden?"

Jolie was about to answer when the front door opened. Footsteps boomed through the house as if a giant had entered.

"What would I have to do?" Jolie asked, her focus divided between this conversation and the thundering footsteps.

"Wear a white gown, cut mistletoe from the branches of the oak and catch it in a white silk scarf, never letting it touch the ground," a man's voice answered.

Chapter Six

Jolie felt as if she'd been thrown face down into a snowdrift, her senses suddenly muffled.

"Oh, there you are, Rory," Mae gushed. "Jolie, this is our teacher and benefactor, the leader of the male side of our Circle."

The man's officious manner and toothy grin did not match what Jolie saw when she looked at him. Why was he here? He didn't belong. The ladies were clean and good, and whole and this man, with the pit-dark eyes, was not.

Beware. There is danger here, a voice in her head warned. She felt the spot between her shoulder blades as if there were a target painted there.

But luckily for Jolie, Rory turned his attention to the ladies. "Ah lovely ladies, I'm charmed." He bowed like some slimy B-movie lord out of an old black and white Robin Hood flick, but Jolie could see that it wasn't Rory who was charmed, it was the coven women. Her eyes flew to Faith's. The old woman had been waiting to see Jolie's reaction.

"I believe you're right, they are under a spell."

Jolie looked from Faith to Rory.

All except you. Jolie could see how the other ladies all had connections to this Rory--like vines twining them together. Only Faith remained separate. Rory glanced at the old woman, and Jolie could see the hate and fear smoldering inside of him. He did not like Faith McBride.

Faith's eyes dropped suddenly, looking like a cat headed for a nap.

"Sean," she purred. "Take Jolie home now, won't you, dear? She has homework to do."

"Sure, Grandma," Sean replied, "As soon as I finish this."

"Now, Sean," Faith's voice bit. "Procrastination is a bad habit. If I died now, you'd feel terrible if you'd denied me my dying wish."

He laughed. "This is your dying wish?"

"Don't be impertinent. You never know. It could be."

"But Rory's here, and we were just about to get started," Mae protested.

Jolie wasn't ready to leave, she had so many questions. But she didn't want to stay near Rory. She looked at Faith.

"Go. Now," Faith commanded.

"I'm sorry, but I really do need to go," Jolie apologized.

"But you will be our maiden, won't you?" Mickey asked, sweetly. "Come early and we can do your hair and...."

"Make sure you've had a bath and removed all those horrid piercings," Mae's thoughts interrupted.

"Sure, she'll do it," Sean replied. "Rick said she would, didn't he?"

Mae's lips tightened at the mention of Rick's name. However much they might differ on the opinions of Rory, neither Faith nor Mae thought much of his egomaniacal groupie.

"Tell your mother not to worry about anything," Iris added. "We have a dress."

"It will be a lovely ceremony," Mae added. "Rory is making all the arrangements."

"Well, that's settled, then. Jolie, give an old woman a kiss," Faith demanded.

Jolie leaned into Faith's powdery cheek.

"You *see* him," Faith whispered. "That's good, but he doesn't *see* you. To him, you're only the child of Rick's girlfriend. Make sure it stays that way. Here, I have something for you." She reached around her neck and drew the chain from it. A small silver woman with her arms raised over her head dangled from the chain. "It's not as powerful as your amulet was when it was fresh, but it will help now." Jolie bent over so Faith could slip the chain over her head. Kissing Jolie softly on the forehead, the frail woman mumbled something Jolie did not catch: A benediction? A prayer? A spell? "Leave it on. It's no good if you're not wearing it," Faith warned. *"Go on home now before they get this farce started. I don't want Rory getting his hooks into you.* Don't worry; we'll see each other again soon."

Jolie followed Sean out, fingering the silver talisman. She could feel the figure's warmth against her chest. Logically it should have been cool from the freezing temperatures as soon as they got outside, but it wasn't. Faith had given Jolie a little bit of herself... "to go".

Sean climbed on his bike and kicked the stand up.

"Crazy old dame, huh?"

"I like her."

"She likes you, too. I can tell. You know, you seemed different in there just now talking to her; softer, sweeter."

"Don't get used to it," Jolie cautioned. "So are you going tomorrow night?"

"Haven't been in years, but there'll be plenty of other people there. It's a local tradition for lots of people around here. Faith's been doing it since before I was born. I think my mother was the original virgin."

Jolie climbed onto the bike and wrapped her arms around his waist. "But you could come this time, couldn't you, Sean?"

Sean laughed. "They aren't going to be putting any beating baby's hearts on the altar or anything, you know, Jo."

With Rory in charge, Jolie wasn't too sure. "It's not my first circus," she bristled. "I've been to more of these things than I like to remember. I hate them. I can never tell the clowns from the tigers."

"Nobody's asking you to walk a tightrope, Jo, and anyway, this time you've got a safety net. Grandma isn't going to let anything happen to you." Sean revved the bike up and pulled it out onto the street.

CHAPTER SEVEN

It was dark by the time Sean turned his bike into the trailer park.

A week before Christmas, there was none of the hustle and bustle you saw in a middle-class neighborhood. If someone wanted to decorate their trailer, it took four dollars and ninety-five cents, five minutes, a chair, and an extension cord. There were no Christmas parties, no baking, no mailing, and any shopping was done at Goodwill or The Dollar Store. People who were lucky enough to be working at all, worked on Christmas, switching shifts with those who actually had family obligations that were more important to them than the extra holiday pay.

If the holidays were the most depressing time of the year, these were the people most depressed: the working poor, the disabled, the alcoholic, the recovering junkie, the old, and the lonely.

Sean's leather-clad back blocked the freezing wind and Jolie's view of her trailer until he made the turn into the park. The park's sadness hit Jolie in the chest with a physical force. The fool that coined the phrase "gifted" for psychics should have been tied to a rock and thrown into a pond to see if he could swim, like they used to do with witches.

"Rick's here," Sean said.

"Yeah, I see." Jolie slid off the bike.

"You don't like him much, do you?"

"I try not to get too attached to Mom's boyfriends. They don't usually stay around too long. Thanks for the ride."

"No problem." Sean shut off the engine and parked his bike, then swung his leg over.

Jolie's internal warning system started ringing off the wall the moment she stepped inside the trailer. You could smell the ozone of violence. Jessie or Rick might ignite it, one playing off the other's lead, taking whichever role was the polar opposite. Suddenly, an arm would swing and one of them would be on the floor with a fat lip or a black eye. The pre-requisite for all Jessie's boyfriends was, they had to know how to play this game.

"Where have you been this time, another concert?" Rick sneered.

Jolie's senses immediately became hyper alert and she pulled her shoulder blades together as if protecting the soft flesh between them.

Sean followed her in. "She was with me."

Bloodshot eyes went from Sean to Jolie. "Slut."

"Hey, that's not called for, Rick," Sean said. "I told you, she was with me."

"Leave it alone, Sean," Jolie warned.

"What? You think I'm blind, man? Is that what you think? You think I haven't seen you giving her the eye?" Rick turned to Jolie. "You don't fool me, miss goodie two shoes. You're as wild as your mother and probably just as hot, once you're engine gets started."

"Lay off her, Rick," Jessie muttered.

"Lay off her? I ain't the one who laid on her. That was Sean here. He's the one you should be nagging. He's spoiled your little girl, Jessie. Don't you care? My god, what kind of a mother are you?"

"Look, if something happened, it's their business. Sean didn't do anything to her she didn't want him to, did you, Sean?"

"I didn't do anything, Jessie; honest."

"He didn't," Jolie backed him up.

Chapter Seven

"You did this on purpose to make me look bad in front of Rory, didn't you?" Rick accused them both. "Not a virgin anymore, are you?"

"This is nuts. We told you, nothing happened. He took me to meet Mae and Faith and the rest of them. We were just there at the house. Call and ask them. They'll tell you."

"I'm not asking those bitches anything."

Sean stepped forward. "Come on, Rick. You're drunk."

"No. I'm not, coming on. We need this settled, right now. Is Jolie a virgin or not?"

"Man, Rick, what is it with you? We told you, nothing happened. I took her to meet the ladies; that's all," Sean insisted.

"Well, I guess there's only one way to find out, isn't there?" Rick pushed himself up from the dinette and stumbled toward Jolie.

"Don't touch me," Jolie warned him.

"Why not? Not good enough for you?"

"Calm down, Rick," Sean stepped forward.

"Oh, let him be, Sean. He's just being an ass," Jessie waved Sean off, drunkenly.

"Stay away from me." Jolie backed up, scanning for a weapon...an escape route, anything to stop the scene she felt coming at them like a freight train, but she was out of time. Rick was coming toward her. Turning, she made a dash for her bedroom as he lunged forward. Missing his mark, he tackled her around her hips, knocking her to the floor. Jolie screamed, her feet scrabbling for traction against the floor tiles.

"What the hell, Rick!" In two steps Sean was in the middle of it.

"Stop it! Stop it, all of you!" Jessie shouted, suddenly jerked out of her alcohol induced complaisance.

"You little bitch!" Rick's arms slipped down the legs of Jolie's jeans, catching on her shoes. Kicking with all her strength, she loosened his grip long enough to sprint for her room. Rick was only a breathe behind her.

"What do you think you're doing? Leave her alone, Rick!" Jessie pushed her way past Sean and vaulted into the chaos, ineffectually trying to pull Rick back and break his focus on her daughter.

"Stay back, Mom," Jolie warned, trying to pull the accordion door to her bedroom shut behind her. Rick's body, wedged between it and the doorjamb, was in the way. "Get away from me you pervert!" She tried to push him out.

"Always so high and mighty, aren't you? You think you got something so much better than any other bitch? Let's have a look."

"Lay a finger on me and I'll cut it off, I swear!"

"Stop him, Sean!" Sean and Jessie tried to pull Rick away. "Please, stop him."

Yanking Rick back by the shoulders and spinning him around, Sean drew back and punched Rick hard in the face. The reincarnation of Simon Magus fell like a sandbag.

Rick looked up from the floor, wiping a trickle of blood from the corner of his mouth. "You gonna fight me, Sean?" He got up. "Okay, I'm with you. Come on. You've been itching for this for a long time, just like you been itching for a piece of that girl."

Sean and Rick eyed each other like they were in some old spaghetti western with Jessie's sobbing providing the soundtrack.

Chapter Seven

Jolie looked around her bedroom. There was only one way in or out, and Rick controlled it. She searched for something she could use to protect herself. Her backpack was in the living room, so she didn't even have a pen. When she turned back to the door, Rick had moved away.

Peeking through the crack in the door, she could only see the bathroom door, but she could hear scuffling noises, punctuated by thuds and Jessie's screams coming from outside. Cautiously, Jolie stepped out of her door.

"Stop! Stop it! Rick…Sean…." Jessie was shouting. Jolie tiptoed up the middle of the trailer until she could see out the front window. She was alone inside now. Everyone else was in the driveway.

Porch lights began coming on in the neighbors' trailers. Rick and Sean would have an audience, but she wouldn't be among them she decided. Whatever happened here tonight, she was done. Jolie grabbed her backpack from the floor where she'd dropped it, slipped out the door and into the darkness.

CHAPTER EIGHT

Jolie felt safer than she should have under the bright lights of the casino. A casino was, after all, a place where people came to indulge, party, gamble, and drink, but in Jolie's experience, most of the horrors done to children happened in the privacy of someone's home and that made this very public place a kind of safety zone.

She considered going to a late movie. It would be dark, and warm, and if she switched theaters a few times she could make it through to the early hours of tomorrow. On the other hand, if she got caught, there would be the inevitable call to the police, followed by a call to Juvenile Probation, and her plan would be screwed before she even knew what it was. Anyway, paying for a movie was something you did if you were planning on going back home later, not if you were running away, and Jolie had decided that was what she was doing: running away.

I'm not going back. Not ever, she told herself, wondering if Sean was all right. She felt crappy about running out on him after he'd stood up for her like that, but she hadn't asked him to lay into Rick, and he must have known what he was doing.

She worried about her mom, too. What would Jessie do when she figured out Jolie was gone? Probably nothing. She'd been drunk when Jolie got home and she'd be drunker before she went to bed. She probably wouldn't even notice Jolie was missing until she got home from work late Friday night or early Saturday morning. And school tomorrow? Who cared? She wasn't going back. The fact that Megan and Brad and their lame

Chapter Eight

clique would think they'd scared her off with that stupid cherry bomb stunt burned her, but not enough to go back. No one, except Becca, would even care she was gone.

Jolie pushed her goal of graduating back to a distant corner of her mind and shoveled mental dirt on it. *Graduating wasn't going to change anything for someone like her*, she told herself. *She'd get a GED someday. That would be good enough. She wasn't going back.*

She noticed a security guard watching her. The hanging out routine worked better when you were small. Then, you could pretend you were lost or had a bad parent who left you while they went off gambling. You could play on people's sympathies. The scenario usually included ice cream. But people had a different attitude when it came to teenagers. Teenagers were suspect like they were expected to be bad. Jolie needed somewhere else to go. She thought about the old homeless radio woman, and wondered where she was sleeping tonight? Probably in one of the storage sheds at the trailer park.

Not an option, Jolie decided. *Too close.* There was nothing for her back at the trailer park. If she and Jessie had stashed their getaway money out in the shed, Jolie might have been tempted to go back for it, but that hadn't happened yet. There was only one thing back there that was of any value to Jolie: Jessie's old phone book. It had the numbers of everyone back in New Orleans--that is if they'd returned to the city and their numbers hadn't changed after Katrina. The problem was: Jolie didn't know where the book was. Her mom had never shown it to her, mentioned it, or even admitted it existed. Jolie had stumbled on it during their last move.

It's probably in one of the boxes in the shed, she thought. But without knowing for sure, going back to hunt for it was risky.

The security guard began walking toward her and Jolie made a show of checking the time on her cell, then looking around like she was waiting for someone. He slowed down, then stopped. After a few minutes, Jolie huffed as if in frustration, and walked away like she was finally giving up. The guard followed her all the way out of the casino, watching her as she crossed the parking lot.

At the edge of the property, Jolie ducked behind a palm tree. It was cold, and time to tally up her resources. Her pockets held a few stray bills and some change. The front pouch of her backpack, where she'd stashed her mom's tips, looked substantial, but tips always looked like more than they really were. A roll might look like a hundred dollars until you counted it and it was all ones. Now, if there were tens, twenties, or even fives in it, it added up nicely, but most people didn't tip that well on this side of town. Jolie opened the wad, flattened it out and counted. There was a little over fifty bucks. It wouldn't get her far.

Dumb, she told herself. Major life decisions, like leaving home, should be planned, but Jolie was too busy proving the adage: children learn what they live, to stop and consider something as practical as consequences. Jolie couldn't name one person she knew who had thought through a pivotal point of their lives: marriage, work, education--and certainly not parenthood. It should have come as no surprise that she'd made her first big decision on impulse. She'd promised herself that she'd never go back, but she was completely unprepared to go forward. What she needed to do, was to stake out the trailer and hope her mom & Rick left, then sneak back in

Chapter Eight

and gather what she needed. The problem was, what if she got caught? Still mulling over the risks, Jolie began to walk down the block.

A white and green sign over a boxy building announced: Bob Allen's Rehearsal Studios. As she got closer, Jolie could see empty beer bottles lined up along the walls to either side of the door, mementos from the bar next door. The iron grates covering the window and door said everything about the neighborhood's respect for property, but rehearsal studios meant bands, and bands meant musicians, and musicians meant late night traffic. There were always people hanging around bands. Nobody would even notice one more.

Jolie approached and tried the door. It was locked. A sign read: buzz to get in. Jolie wondered how many of the studio's patrons took it literally, but she didn't dare push the button. Questions might be asked and she wasn't ready for questions. She had no answers.

Deciding to run away had seemed so logical at the moment, but leaving home, even a bad one, brought a new set of problems. Instinct had told Jolie to put space between herself and the danger of Rick's and Sean's fight. The ever-present fantasy of being on her own was seductive; the reality, however, was not. The decisions she needed to make suddenly loomed large. One bad choice, one wrong move, or misplaced trust, and all her choices could vanish. Human trafficking was alive and well in Sin City, and its streets were no place for a girl alone.

Jolie pulled her coat tight around her and leaned back against the iron bars, shaking. She felt like someone had stripped the varnish from her and peeled all the paint off, leaving her all raw and scratched up. She needed some space and a little time to pull herself back together.

A scrawny twenty-something with long hair came out of the studio, a pair of drumsticks sticking out of his back pocket.

"Thanks, man." Jolie flashed him a smile as she ducked under his arm.

The place smelled like stale cigarettes, illicit beer, and illegal herbs. The sign on the vintage sixties industrial style desk read: no alcohol, which was probably easier to enforce than if it had read: no pot, which might have folded the place. The rest of the reception area was a steel tub, framed genuine leatherette covered couch that had as much duct tape as vinyl on its cushions; a steel legged side table covered with cup stains and old magazines, and a wall covered with old posters from bands and acts that had once played Vegas. Loud music blasted from two of the studios down the hall. Signed eight by ten glossy photographs of bands and acts that had, presumably, rehearsed there sometime during the last fifty years, papered both sides of the hallway. Jolie had never heard of any of them. Rehearsing didn't guarantee a band was any good, and even if they were, that didn't guarantee they'd be recognizable to a kid her age. Some of them were pretty funny looking with their "mod" clothes and funny haircuts, but at least the ones from the sixties were recognizable as people. The eighties punk bands and glam, rock groups looked like a bad designer's idea of high fashion from another planet.

Jolie walked down the narrow hall looking at the photos and trying to listen at the different rehearsal rooms; searching for one that was empty. The silent ones were locked. She headed back to the torn vinyl couch in the lobby. Opting to hide in plain sight, she curled up with her coat on and pulled her hood down over her head. A girl waiting for a musician was as common as a gambler waiting for tokens. Everyone would assume she was with someone else.

"Kid, what are you doing here?" A man's voice woke her.

Balled up in a fetal position with her knees tight against her chest, it took Jolie a minute to remember where she was.

"Waiting," she answered, peeling her cheek from the vinyl couch, and trying to wipe off the wet spot where she'd drooled.

"Waiting for who?" the guy asked.

Shit, Jolie thought. *Say something. Think.* She sat up slowly and rubbed her eyes, buying time. "Eddie? He's with the band."

"Which band?"

Jolie looked down the hall. "The one down there," she said, vaguely.

"There's no one left here but us. Hey, one of you guys know an Eddie in the other band here tonight?" the guy called back into studio one.

No one did.

"Oh man. He dumped me," Jolie complained petulantly. "That jerk. I can't believe it. He was my ride. What a shit."

"Where're you going?" the big man asked.

"I was gonna crash at Eddie's place."

"Where's that?"

She was in improv mode now, and she had no idea where it would take her. Jolie fumbled in her backpack and found the crumpled piece of paper Ms. Warren had given her with the paranormal guy's address on it. She picked a number that was five numbers off the one written there just to be safe.

"Thirty-two Forty Oak, BC. What's BC?"

"Boulder City. Come on. We live out that way. We'll give you a ride."

Jolie sized him up, wishing her gift would kick in. It didn't. She didn't like hitchhiking. You never knew what you were getting into, or with who. Walking might take longer, but you had a better chance of getting where you were going.

A woman with short-cropped burgundy hair, wearing a long peasant skirt and boots came out of the studio.

"Ready, Marty?" she asked, digging for something in an oversized drawstring bag.

"Hey, Tru, is it okay if we give the kid here a ride? Some jerk stranded her."

Tru looked Jolie over. "I guess. She doesn't look like she could cause too much trouble."

"That's what I thought when I first picked you up." Marty grinned. "And look where that got me." He was no rock star. He probably wasn't even a working musician, and there was no telling what the flamboyant Tru was.

Tru poked Marty's pillow-belly.

"It just goes to show you can't tell by looking, huh babe?" Marty put his arm around Tru's shoulders and planted a kiss on her lips.

"You coming, kid?" Tru asked as they headed out. "It's gettin' early."

Jolie grabbed her stuff and followed them to a beat up old fifty-seven Dodge pickup; old being the definitive word.

"It needs a little paint." Marty patted the hood. "But it's got a new engine, brakes, tranny…all the stuff that counts. Paint's just cosmetic."

"Like lipstick," Tru added. "It goes on last and you don't always need it."

Chapter Eight

Jolie figured it needed a lot more than paint, but she didn't say so.

"So where are you headed this time of night?" Tru asked once they'd fished out an extra seat belt from behind the bench seat and settled in.

Jolie clung to the passenger side door, trying not to touch Tru. She didn't want to know things she shouldn't. She held the paper up to the street light, trying to avoid the shadow made by the crystal pendulum hanging from the rear-view mirror. "Thirty-two forty Oak. That's the address Eddie gave me."

"Oak, huh?" True frowned, didn't say anything and they pulled out onto the highway. "So, this Eddie, who is he to you?"

"He was just sort of helping me out."

Tru nodded. "Do you have any money?"

Uh-oh, here it comes, Jolie thought. "A little," she said carefully.

"Enough?"

"Know anyone who does?"

Marty chuckled. Don't worry; we're not interested in your money, kid."

"So where are your folks?" Tru asked.

Jolie shrugged.

"Do they know where you are?"

Jolie didn't answer.

"Don't you think they'll be worried?"

"Look, you offered me a ride. If I'd known you wanted my life story, I'd have said no. What's the deal, are you practicing to be a social worker, or trying to write a book or something?"

"Or something."

"You don't have to get mean," Marty said. "Tru's just got a big heart. She's just trying to look after you, is all."

"Thanks, but I've already got a mother."

"I'm not applying for the job," Tru said. "I just thought it seemed like maybe you could use some help."

"I've had enough of that today, thanks."

"If this guy, Eddie, dumped you at the studio, maybe going to his place isn't such a good idea," Marty added.

Jolie could see the logic. She hadn't thought her story out very well. It was making her look dumb. "If I can get there, there'll be someone..." she left the thought hanging.

Tru looked out the window and let the silence sit.

"The first time I ran away, I was twelve," she said after awhile.

"A late starter, huh?" Marty chuckled.

"It's not about where or when you start, it's about how it ends," Tru defended herself. "Some kids are lucky and they get it out of their systems, their parents find them, or they end up in a good group home, and they're okay. Others end up drugged out, or hookin', or dead. It's hard for girls on the street--sometimes even harder when they get the wrong kind of help. They get picked up and shipped off overseas, or some pimp gets his hooks into them and they're used up before they're old enough to get a legal drink."

Jolie sighed. "Look, you don't know anything about my life. So I'd appreciate it if you'd quit trying to spoon feed me what you think I ought to do with it."

"Sorry. You're right. It's none of my business. It's just that I kind of figure we're all responsible for each other, you know?"

"Not really." But Jolie did know. She just didn't want to think about it, and Tru was making her do just that.

Chapter Eight

They drove on to the sound of the pick-up's big V-8. As the engine heated up, the cab got warmer. Even so, Tru stayed snuggled up to Marty. He wasn't a handsome guy, though he might have been seventy-five pounds ago, but he was cute in a cuddly bear sort of a way.

Jolie liked the way he'd stood up for Tru. If you looked at them as separate people, you might wonder what someone like Tru saw in a guy like Marty, but if you saw them together, it was clear they belonged. He was a good guy, and he was crazy about her, and that was more important than all the hunky bad boy bullshit Hollywood tried to sell to girls.

Marty slowed down as he drove into Boulder. After a few turns, he pulled over to the curb.

"Should be somewhere around here." He peered out of the window. There were a few old houses that looked like they'd been remodeled into apartments and a big old church on the corner. "What was that number again?" Marty asked.

Jolie checked the number on the paper. It matched the number on the church.

"Look, I don't see any thirty-two forty, kid. Are you sure you got it right?"

"I don't know. Eddie wrote it down. Maybe he lied."

"Look, isn't there someplace else we can take you?"

Jolie felt the silver talisman against her chest. "Do you know where Cedar Street is?"

"Yeah."

"There's a house there, maybe I could go to."

"What's the number?"

"I don't know, but I'll know it when I see it."

Marty and Tru exchanged glances. He pulled back out and drove on. The windows were fogging up. Jolie rolled hers down so she could see. The air was really cold, and like a slap in the face, it helped push her emotions back.

The houses they passed were all dark, except for those that had left their Christmas lights on. Jolie watched them go by, looking for Mae's. When she saw it, she started to tell Marty to stop, then thought better of it. If he and Tru got a twinge of conscience, it would be better if they didn't know where she'd gone. She pointed down the street.

"That one there," she said.

"It's dark. No one's up," Marty said.

"That's all right. I know where they keep the spare key," she lied, hopping out of the truck.

"You want us to wait till you get in, just in case?"

"No. It's okay. I'm sorry about what I said, Tru. I really do appreciate your help."

Tru shook her head. "No problem."

"I'll be okay, really," Jolie assured her. "Thanks for the ride."

"Take care of yourself, kid." Marty smiled.

Jolie pretended to head toward the back of the house, hiding behind a bush until the truck drove away, then she headed back up the street toward Aunt Mae's.

CHAPTER NINE

As Jolie tip-toed through the stiff grass, the sound of its crunching bouncing off the block wall that separated Mae's yard from the neighbors, she wondered if the coven ladies really knew anything about magic, or if they were just bored women playing at being something they thought was exciting. Faith seemed real enough but Jolie had barely met the others, and she couldn't understand how, if they had any talents at all, they'd been taken in by a pretender like Rory. The other thing that bugged her was; if Faith saw through his act, why hadn't she exposed Rory to the others? It didn't make sense. Jolie dismissed her confusion. Most of the grown up world didn't make sense to her.

Jolie expected that if any of the ladies did know anything about protection, there would be some kind of ward around the house and yard. In that case, they would know pretty soon that she was out here. She walked on, not seeing or feeling anything. Even the seasonal holly and ivy above the door seemed purely decorative--after all, it had let Rory in and apparently Rick, too. Did any of this magic stuff work at all? She touched the amulet Faith had given her. It still felt warm and comforting, but was it warm because it had been next to her body, and felt comforting to her because she liked the old woman who had given it to her? Was that all a magical protection was, a psychological placebo?

Mem had done house blessings and protections for her own and other people's homes. Jolie had even gone along a few times and she remembered how good and energetically clean the places felt when Mem was done but did that prove anything? Wasn't it just as likely that Mem's family and friends thought of her as a source of goodness? Jolie remembered seeing glistening dust clouds of energy flowing from the lines her grandmother drew around her house, but five-year-olds were impressionable and had a flexible sense of reality-- almost as flexible as an eighty-year-old woman who believed her family had special gifts and knowledge.

Looking at the whole thing logically, it was embarrassing and dumb to admit you believed it. How could what magic workers claimed they were doing really work? Did a little bell or buzzer go off in the spell caster's head when the ward they had set was broken? And who was an intruder, the neighbor boy getting his ball out of your yard? The gardener? Was it only the intent that made the difference? It couldn't be real and yet Jolie had seen something encircling those houses Mem had blessed. In spite of the brief encouragement she'd felt after meeting Faith, Jolie just wasn't sure what she believed anymore. If there were secrets to the universe and she was supposed to be party to them, then why was her life such a mess? And if her experiences were real, and she was not crazy, did that validate all claims of magic by others? Jolie couldn't remember ever being any other way than how she was, and she had struggled throughout her childhood to understand how other people experienced the world, but what they saw and what she saw were so different, they seemed like two completely different places. In a world where everything was divided into right and wrong, someone had to be wrong, didn't they?

Walking the length of Mae's house, Jolie tried to remember its layout from her brief visit. The ground floor bedrooms would come off the hall that led to the back. She hadn't seen any doors, but doors were what

Chapter Nine

gave a hall purpose, so there had to be some. The first window she came to would be the living room. It was a large plate glass affair and she recognized the flowery chintz drapes. The next window had to be in the kitchen. When Faith had sent Sean to eat there, he'd gone through a swinging door to the right: the North side of the house. This window was one of those little garden add-ons that people gave women for Mother's Day and installed over the sink so the woman could pretend to enjoy doing dishes; like someone was giving them permission to daydream as long as they stayed on the job. It was a half step above giving your mom a vacuum cleaner in Jolie's book.

A dog barked somewhere close by and Jolie stopped, listening warily. The animal was on the other side of the block wall, unable to cause her a problem. She moved on. Pushing through the bushes, she checked the next window. The blind was closed--a good sign that it was a bedroom, but was it Faith's? She imagined Mae's reaction at being woken up in the middle of the night by Jolie knocking on her window. Would she call Jessie Lynn or Rick? Probably. Faith might not be crazy about a mid-night visit, but once Jolie explained things, Faith would understand.

Jolie slid her body along the outside wall of the house, trying not to think about spiders or scorpions as the branches swept across her back. The next window had no blind. Holding onto the outside ledge, Jolie braced her feet against the house and pulled herself up to see in.

It was dark inside, except for the faint blue glow from a computer screen. Probably an office, Jolie thought, certainly not Faith's room. Letting herself down, she almost jumped out of her skin as something furry brushed against her leg.

"Oh my God!"

Yellow eyes peered from the shadows and Jolie could barely see the outline of a cat against the darkness. The cat gave Jolie the once over then dismissed her, silently padding off toward the garden shed in the backyard.

"Dumb cat," she muttered, turning back to the problem of locating Faith. She pressed past the bush on the back corner and stepped out into the open yard, heading for the other side of the house. She was midway across the lawn when something in the garden shed fell, clattering, then rolling on the ground. Jolie stopped again, waiting. When no lights came on, and no one appeared to challenge her, she continued.

The South side of the house was just as dark and brushy as the North. Jolie swept the branches aside and pushed herself through to the wall. Rising onto tiptoes, she peered in. There were fewer windows on this side. Besides the ones she could account for as living room and dining room at the front, there was only a small one high up the wall; a bathroom, she decided. The one window remaining had blinds pulled almost all the way down. Jolie tried to peek under but there was no light. She closed her eyes, counted to sixty, then opened them again. Laid out over a chair, she could see Mae's dress, the white lace collar glowing against the navy background. *Mae's dress, Mae's room.* Jolie headed back around to the North side of the house.

Something rustled in the shed and a light flared inside, hissing with the soft shush of a propane lantern. Jolie froze. The cat stood just outside the edge of the light's circle facing the open door, its spine arched, its hair on end. It added its hiss to the propane's, not just a single warning but a long, slow, threat, like a lifeboat springing a leak. What did it see that threatened it so?

Chapter Nine

Jolie tiptoed forward. A cold sweat broke out under her winter clothes, but it did not stop her curiosity.

There was someone inside the shed, talking quietly. Were they talking to the cat? Jolie could not tell, but whatever they were saying, the cat wasn't going for it. It stayed where it was, still hissing. Jolie felt a slimy creepiness and reconsidered her thoughts about the cat's intelligence. The animal was right; something strange was going on in Mae's backyard. Jolie crept forward. Keeping to one side of the door, she stretched out her neck to see around the corner.

A male figure squatted in the middle of the floor. She could not see his face, only his knees, his hands, and the spell-circle he was drawing around himself. A dark candle stood in the center of the circle, and he was mumbling words she couldn't hear. She didn't need to. She could feel the energy moving.

The cat looked up and gave a questioning meow. Instantly, the man stopped, listening to the night, the air, and the stillness surrounding the house.

Jolie breathed slowly through her nose, her face pointed away from the door's opening so he would not hear her, or see her breath in the freezing air. The shushing sound of pants brushing together moved toward the door, and she pressed herself back against the wall, slinking toward the rear of the building, trying to balance her need for silence with her desire for speed. She was slipping around the back corner when the man cleared the shed door.

He looked toward the house and waited, but it was dark and quiet; everyone inside still fast asleep. The neighbor's dog barked again. The cat leaped from cover, sprinting across the yard to the back steps. A pile of terra cotta pots stacked on the patio toppled, cracking with hollow popping sounds. Two pots rolled across the walkway. The neighbor's dog went nuts, joined by another several houses away. A light switched on at the house between them.

"Shut up, ya dumb dog," a man shouted, angrily.

Jolie stood like an escaped prisoner, exposed in a spotlight. Shielded from the man in the shed by the shed's walls, she was completely visible to the angry neighbor. Slowly, she slid down the shed wall until she was crouched in the shadow of the block wall between them. Staying hunched over, she ran through the graveyard of abandoned junk behind the shed, toward the safety of deeper shadows.

"Hey, what's with the barking, Buddy?" a sleepy voice next door asked, groggily. "People are trying to sleep, dude. Come on, settle down." The dog's owner let it in, then slid the door shut behind them. The lights in both of the disturbed houses went off. The other dog stopped barking and the night became quiet once again.

"Damn cat," the man in the shed muttered as he turned to go back inside.

Jolie sucked in a cold breath, her heart stumbling over itself. She knew that voice: it was Sean's. This wasn't creepy Rory or evil Rick, it was Sean--her Sean; Faith's grandson. What was he doing working secret spells in the middle of the night in his aunt's shed?

It couldn't be him, she told herself. Jolie waited to be sure the man had returned his attention to his task, then crept forward and peered around the edge of the doorway. The spell caster had shifted his position so that his body faced the door. If he looked up he would see her. Jolie pulled back, flattening herself against the wall and tried to catch her breath.

It was Sean. How could it be Sean? Her head reeled, dizzy with confusion. Did she really not know him at all? She had always considered herself a good judge of character, but then, she had been comparing herself to Jessie Lynn who was a disaster. All her old questions about why someone like Sean would hang out with someone like Rick returned. Sometimes good people just made bad friendships, didn't they? It didn't make them bad people. Sean's own grandmother had called him a bad boy, but Jolie hadn't thought she really meant it. She struggled for understanding, but the feeling that she had been betrayed stampeded in, overriding everything. *Stupid, stupid, stupid.* How could she have broken her own rule? How could she have trusted him?

Carefully retracing her steps, Jolie made her way around to the back side of the shed, through the stacks of leftover building materials, rusty wheelbarrow parts, bicycles, and yard debris.

Something slunk low to the ground through and below the obstacle course of junk.

The cat, Jolie thought, hoping the silly thing wasn't going to get her discovered.

"What are you doing?" a voice startled her from behind.

Jolie spun around.

There was no one there. No one had seen her. She had not been found. The dark thing hiding in the junk moved again. Standing on its hind feet, it leaped onto the roof. Like a crab, it ran up to the peak then skittered on all fours down the far side. The oily feeling on her skin, that always came with the ink blot creature that hung around Rick, slid over her, and she felt nauseous, her skin alive with strange sensations, her eyes seeing the edges of the world with alarming sharpness. Something was wrong.

Stepping carefully through the discarded junk, Jolie tiptoed back to where she could see inside the shed door.

E.F. Winters

The yard was dark, except for the light streaming from the shed, but it felt as if something evil were watching from the sidelines, preparing to pounce. It was.

Rick's silhouette stood in front of Sean, blocking her view of the inside of the shed.

"Haven't you done enough for one night?" Sean said wearily.

"You're an idiot," Rick snarled. "What do you think you're doing here?"

Oh God, were they going to fight again? Here? Now? Using Rick's body as cover, Jolie ran for the security of the bushes by the house. Safe within the bushes' embrace, she sucked deep full breaths of air. It left a bitter taste at the back of her throat. *What was going on?* She wanted to scream, but she did not dare. The terror rising inside her had no logical root, but it felt very real.

Then she saw it; a black fog was rolling slowly across the grass toward the house. The cat stepped out from the shrubbery opposite her and froze, its eyes fixed on the same approaching darkness. Slowly, the cat began backing away; lifting its paws high as if the stuff was water it didn't want to touch.

"Here kitty, kitty, kitty," Jolie called in a whisper. The fog was almost on it when the cat let out a feline shriek and bolted.

That was it. Jolie had seen enough. She made a fist, reached up and banged on Faith's window as hard as she could.

"Faith!" she shouted. "Get up! Get up now!"

Instantly, the two men were at the door of the shed.

"Jolie? Jolie is that you?" Sean called out.

Rick jumped forward like a coiled snake, striking across the lawn toward her. "Fucking bitch." She felt a hot, sharp stab of pain between her shoulder blades as if all Rick's malevolent thoughts were a knife, and he was sticking it into her.

"Faith, wake up, now! You're in danger!" Jolie screamed then turned and ran.

CHAPTER TEN

Jolie knew there was no such thing as fast enough when all you had were two legs and what was chasing you had five hundred horsepower under the hood. The odds were not going to be fair. Setting herself a pace she knew she could not maintain, she could only hope that chance would throw her a bone before she ran out of steam. The engine of Rick's El Camino revved up behind her. She resisted the urge to look back. If she'd learned anything from watching a half hundred bad horror movies, it was that you didn't look back. That, and you never, ever, wore heels when there was any chance of getting chased by the undead. She couldn't be sure if the feet she heard pounding the pavement behind her were someone else's, or the echo of her own. Breathing hard, she tried to find a rhythm matching her breath to her feet.

Behind her, Rick's truck roared like a demon.

She needed to get off the street. She began watching the yards on her right as she ran, searching for one that had a clear shot at the alley that divided the block. At the first open yard, she veered to the right. The suburban yard, with its abandoned icons of childhood: the broken swing, sun-bleached trampoline, and frostbitten garden, was unsettling in its silence. Jolie let herself through a back gate and came out in the alley. Scanning up and down the narrow lane, she looked for her next move. A second, smaller engine started up and approached the alley in the opposite direction from Rick's truck.

Sean. It had to be Sean. If he and Rick worked together they'd put her right between them, cornering

Chapter Ten

her. He had stood up against Rick to protect her, why would he help Rick now? He had to know that Rick meant her no good.

Jolie's side ached. *Wimp*, she taunted herself. *You might as well be screaming your lungs out in those damn heels,* but she wouldn't be able to run much longer. She had to find someplace to hide, and she had to find it fast.

She considered the rows of backyards, hoping a plan would miraculously pop up. Sean's motorcycle had the speed of a car with the advantage of maneuverability, but it could not climb fences. Still, there couldn't be any halfway about such a move. It was all or nothing because getting caught with her back side sprawled across a fence, her skivvy-clad buns wriggling in the air, was definitely a recipe for trouble.

Sean's bike turned into the alley and began driving toward her. Pro and con time was over. Jolie scrambled over the fence and fell into the yard on the other side. The streak of movement and the snarl that followed didn't register until the dog's teeth sank into her calf.

"Ow! Shit!" Jolie cursed, still running. The pain caught up with her after she'd dragged the mutt halfway across the yard. Her body gave an instinctive jerk, twisting her leg out of the animal's clenched teeth. "Get off me, you damn mutt!" Her jeans made a long tearing sound as she vaulted over the fence that fronted the street side of the house. The dog and half her pants stayed behind.

"Jolie! Are you all right?" Sean called from the alley.

No, I am not, you douche bag, she thought, but she didn't say it out loud. She had too many questions and too little trust. Was the black fog still moving toward Mae's house? What would it do when it got there? Had Sean summoned it?

No, she told herself, as she ran. Sean would never put his grandmother in danger. But if he was such a good guy, why was he chasing her when he should have been trying to help Mae and Faith? And if Sean wasn't who she thought he was, and she was wrong...? God, she wished she knew what he had been doing in that shed.

Jolie crossed the front yard, then the street, and jumped up onto a porch with a half wall and ducked down behind it. Her leg burned like a hell hound had left coals in her flesh. She sieved a breath through her teeth and listened for the dog. She could hear it huffing and whining, but it couldn't get to her. Limping to the far end of the porch, Jolie swung her legs over and dropped into the yard on the other side, trying to take the weight on her good leg. The damaged one hurt like hell, but adrenaline was in charge now. Crossing the adjacent backyard, she found herself in the alley one block over from where she'd started.

The far side was heavily overgrown. Piles of leaves and debris were sitting like beached whales at the foot of a high rock wall with ivy pouring over it. Un-pruned for years, the vines stretched across the alley, reaching for the other side. The beam of Sean's headlight shone through the slats of a street-side fence, flashing light and dark, like a ship's SOS.

"Jo? Jolie? Where are you?" Jolie could hear Sean calling her over the engine noise. It wouldn't take him long to figure out where she'd gone. Rick's El Camino rumbled as it worked its way around the block. She would not be alone much longer.

The steeple of a church rose above her, standing out against the night sky. Its foundation had to be connected to whatever was on the other side of the ivy-covered wall: a church or graveyard. Jolie didn't care which. She had more to fear from the living now than the dead at the

Chapter Ten

moment. Sean's lights disappeared from the street, circling to the North side of the block while Rick's truck approached from the South. In a minute, they'd be at either end of the alley and if she stayed where she was, she'd be exposed in their headlights like a doomed rabbit. A gust of wind rustled the ivy, revealing a hollow space behind it. Jolie took one last look up and down the alley and dove through the curtain of leaves. They closed behind her.

Inching along the wall, Jolie moved deeper into the heart of the old vine as the buzz of Sean's bike got closer, slowing as he searched for her. The El Camino joined the party, vibrating the alley so that the ivy danced. Jolie held her breath as the two vehicles passed each other, turned, then returned, changing sides, their headlights acting like huge flashlights. She could hear the men shouting at each other, but could not make out what they said. Wishing she could sink into the wall and disappear, she leaned back. The wall moved. Careful not to stir the leaves, Jolie's fingers crawled across the surface behind her, feeling the texture. There was rock, then an edge, a latch, and wood. *It's a gate.*

Oh, please, please, let it open, Jolie begged, pressing her weight against the wooden slats. It gave a few inches, and then a few more. Letting all of the air out of her lungs, Jolie squeezed through as Sean's headlight's passed over the spot she had just left.

CHAPTER ELEVEN

Jolie gulped air as the rumble of engines circled just beyond the curtain of ivy. Finally, unable to find any trace of her, the search moved on.

With her adrenaline level falling, Jolie began feeling her leg. It burned, and a sticky red line ran along her lower calf, dripping into her shoe. She used her hands to gently explore the wound. It was bleeding, but not heavily. Whatever attention it needed could wait. She looked around, taking stock of where her impulsive move had landed her.

It was a square courtyard, sunk below the level of the main church building. The stone walls on the church side rose several stories high, blending into the structure of the church building itself. It might have been pretty during another season, but in winter, it looked like a nightmare version of the Red Queen's garden from Alice in Wonderland: all thorny with wild twisted seedpods growing in blatant scorn of any notion of flowerbeds. The woody knots of rosebushes and chopped off branches of dead trees repeated a common story in Southern Nevada; transplants did not thrive here. Planting water-loving plants in the Mojave Desert was a popular mistake for newcomers, who packed their favorite flowers and shrubs along with the sweaters and boots they would soon discard.

Built into the church side wall, a set of stairs led up to a back door two stories above the level of the garden. The glint of glass at the base of the church hinted at a basement.

Chapter Eleven

Jolie shivered. The sweat she'd worked up running was cooling quickly in the night air. She limped through the tall grass, up the back steps, and tried the knob. *Locked.* Limping back down the stairs, Jolie made her way through the overgrown briars and dead grass to the basement window she'd seen. These too were locked.

So much for trusting your fellow man, Jolie thought sullenly. She examined the building's outline. The bell tower, with its belfry at the top, was not fully enclosed, but it would be better than being out here in the open, and she liked the idea that she could see what was going on outside the church walls without anyone seeing her.

Walking along the building's base, Jolie found an arched door and another set of steps leading up. A third of the way up the steps split; one set continuing to the belfry, the second going off toward a secondary part of the church. Jolie took the stairs to the belfry.

Once at the top, she could look out over the neighborhood. Sean's and Rick's headlights were circling several blocks away. Moving to the next window she looked toward where she thought Aunt Mae's must be.

A dull black hole stood out among the other houses. The area had been so completely covered that you couldn't even tell there was a house there. Jolie began to shake. She couldn't breathe--she couldn't even think. She clutched the silver goddess hanging at her neck.

Faith, help me. Jolie bit her lip, spun, and began racing down the stairs. Taking the other set of stairs, she threw herself at the door.

"Help! Please, I need help!" She pounded on the heavy wood. "Wake up! Wake up!"

A light came on inside and after a few minutes the door slowly opened.

"How did you get in there?" a gruff voice demanded, sleepily. "Don't you know it's the middle of the night? Decent people are asleep." The man had to be at least seventy with a face so full of down-trending wrinkles that it looked like he had frowned his whole life.

"I'm sorry, but I need help," Jolie stammered.

"Confession is at eight," the man informed her.

"I'm not here to confess. I need real help," Jolie insisted.

The man's eyebrows rose. "Come back in the morning like everybody else. Father Owen is asleep."

"But by then it could be too late!" Jolie protested.

"Too late for what?" A second man came out of one of the rooms several doors down, wrapping his robe around him. "What's going on, Gibbons?"

"It's some girl, Father Owen. She was at the back door making a ruckus. I don't know how she got in the courtyard."

"I came in from the alley, through the gate." Jolie stepped inside into the light.

"*Dear God!*" Both men's eyes registered shock and surprise.

Jolie looked down and realized what she must look like with her ripped pants, blood dripping down her leg, her face, and neck stained with sweat and dust.

"You're hurt," Father Owen exclaimed.

"A dog bit me," Jolie said, lamely. The men waited for more. "Some men were chasing me so I jumped a fence and a dog bit me."

"Men? Who? The police?" Gibbons demanded. "Why are they after you?"

Jolie tried to think fast. They could put Rick away for the rest of his life, and she'd march in the parade, but she had to believe there was some reasonable explanation for what Sean had done.

"I don't know," she lied.

Father Owen studied her. "You don't live around here, do you? What are you doing running around this neighborhood in the middle of the night?"

"Trying to get some help. He called you Father Owen--James Owen?"

The man nodded. "Yes."

"Ms. Warren from my school gave me your number." Jolie fumbled in her backpack for the piece of paper Ms. Warren had given her. "She said you knew things." Jolie glanced at the other guy, Gibbons, as she handed the paper over as proof, afraid to say too much. "I'm a student at Chaparral and I've been having some problems. Ms. Warren thought you might be able to help me."

Father Owen took the note and looked it over. "Come into my office. I'll take a look at that leg and we can talk. It's all right, Gibbons, you can go back to bed."

Father Owen's office was a small, narrow box with a high ceiling that dwarfed the room. It was more like a closet with a stove, a table, and two chairs than a room, really, with long dusty drapes hanging from a set of tall narrow windows. The priest opened a cupboard and got out a first aid kit.

"Now what is this all about, Miss...?"

"Jolie."

Jolie," he repeated. "Do you have a last name, Jolie?" She didn't answer. "You asked me for help. It would be nice to know how to address you."

"Jolie's enough."

"All right. Can you tell me what sort of trouble you think you're in, Jolie? This may sting a bit." Father

Owen sprayed some antiseptic on the bite then dabbed on ointment.

"Ms. Warren said you were an expert on the occult."

"I've studied it a bit and I wrote a book some years ago. I wouldn't say that makes me an expert."

"But you know something about it? You've seen things?"

Father Owen frowned. "What is this all about?"

Jolie took a long breath then let it out. "I think it would be easier if I showed you, Father. We can see it from the bell tower."

Father Owen got up and pulled a coat from the back of the door. "All right."

Jolie led him out the door and back up the tower stairs. After the warmth of his office, the cold was like needles pricking her skin. She had no idea how to explain to this stranger what she had seen. She could only hope that when she showed him the black fog, he would know what to do.

At the top of the stairs, Jolie crossed to the West side of the tower. "There." She pointed.

The El Camino and Sean's motorcycle were gone, and the neighborhood street silent and still below them. "See that dark spot three blocks over, in the middle; the old bungalow with all the bushes?"

"Mae McBride's?"

Jolie looked at him in surprise.

"We live in the same neighborhood. Mae and I have known each other a long time."

"So, you see it?"

"The house?"

"Yes."

"It's dark."

"Exactly. So you don't see it, really. You just know it's there. Don't you think that's weird?"

Chapter Eleven

Father Owen shook his head. "Did Miss Warren send you to me because of Mae's little 'ladies club'? Is that what this is about? I assure you, Jolie, the ladies are harmless."

They may be, but there's a guy with them who's not. "Look, Father Owen, see how it's all black over there--really black? It's too black, don't you see that?"

"It's nearly three in the morning. People have turned off their lights and gone to bed. There's nothing unusual about that."

Jolie gritted her teeth. She had been so stupid, thinking someone like this was going to see anything important. "You don't see anything out of the ordinary, do you?"

"What I see is a girl with a vivid imagination whose been traumatized by a frightening experience. Did they hurt you?" he asked, clearly trying to be sensitive.

Jolie wanted to slap him. "No. It's not me It's Mae and Faith."

"What were you doing wandering around the streets in the middle of the night on a school night, Jolie?"

It doesn't matter! See wanted to scream. She took a breath and tried again. "Please listen to me, Father Owen. This is important. There is something very wrong at the McBride's. I saw something, like a black fog coming toward the house..."

"Whatever's troubling you, you are in the house of the Lord now, Jolie. You don't have to be afraid here. Nothing can hurt you here."

Nothing except your disbelief, Jolie shouted silently. *Patience.* "I'm not afraid--not for me anyway, and I'm not lying or imagining it. Faith and Mae McBride are in danger."

"Faith and Mae are sound asleep in their beds," Father Owen insisted.

E.F. Winters

"Not anymore. I banged on the window to wake them up when I saw the fog coming. Every light in that house should be on right now, and look at it, it's so black it looks like there's a hole in the world there." Jolie stopped. She could see the look on Father Owens' face. She wasn't convincing him of anything, except that she was nuts. *Damn know-it-all old men*, she swore silently. Straight and narrow guys from Father Owen's generation had very limited ways of dealing with women, and being young only made it worse. As far as a man like this was concerned her brain was as underdeveloped as her breasts. There was really only one way she knew to get to him.

"I'm sorry," Jolie hung her head. "You're probably right, Father. I just can't get it out of my head that something terrible has happened to them." She blinked her eyes, trying to get real tears going, and thought about when she had first learned that Mem had died. Method acting they'd called it in her one acting class. You drew from your own life experiences to get the emotion you wanted. Crying had never been a problem for Jolie; she had plenty to draw from.

"Please." She blinked her eyes tearfully. "Maybe you could just call them and make sure they're alright?"

"It's very late," Father Owen said.

"Maybe we could just drive by the house then, and check to see if everything is okay? It would make me feel so much better."

"In a few hours, it will be morning."

"They could be dead by morning!" Jolie howled, hiding her face in her hands. It was classic Hollywood damsel in distress stuff.

"There, there, Jolie. It's all right," Father Owen tried to calm her. "No one is going to die. You're just imagining things."

Chapter Eleven

Jolie wanted to kick him in the balls. Instead, she looked up at him, tears streaking her face. "You're probably right, Father, but what if I'm not? What if, tomorrow morning we find out that someone murdered them in their beds-- like an ax murderer or something?" The ax murderer bit might have been overdoing it because Father Owen suddenly looked really alarmed.

"You say you were there at the house tonight?"

Jolie nodded. He was re-examining the blood on her clothes.

"Yes, and then the fog..."

"The black fog came and you knew it meant death?"

She heard the suspicion in his voice, but it was too late to change direction.

"Yeah. That's right; the black fog meant death."

"Tell me what you remember about being at Mae's."

"I already told you everything I remember."

"So the black fog came. Then what happened?"

Jolie shrugged. "I screamed, banged on the window, and ran."

Father Owen studied her face carefully. "I see." He frowned. "Well, perhaps it would be wise to make a call, just to be safe. First, let's get you back inside where it's warm. You're freezing."

Father Owen showed Jolie to a small, plain bedroom with a small window. A bedside table, a lamp, and a bible were all that were in it and all there was room for.

"Why don't you sit here and rest that leg? I'll be right back." He closed the door. The keyhole rattled.

"Hey! What are you doing?" Jolie jumped up and threw herself at the door. The priest had locked it. "Hey, open up!" She beat at the door. "What do you think you're doing? You can't keep me in here. Open the door!"

E.F. Winters

"It's for your own safety, Jolie. I think we both need to find out exactly what has happened at the McBride's and what it is that you've done. You just wait here while I have a look. I'm sure everything will be fine, but as you said, it's better to be sure."

"Yeah, right. Everything is going to be just great," Jolie muttered.

The ax murderer thing had definitely been too much.

CHAPTER TWELVE

A cold dawn woke Jolie. She didn't need a clock to tell her it was time for school; her internal alarm clock did that. But she wouldn't be at school today or anytime soon. As soon as she got out of here and made sure Faith was all right, she was headed for New Orleans. She wasn't dropping out. She'd finish high school, just not here. Her phone buzzed from her pocket. It was a text from Becca.

"Where are you? Are you ever going to talk to me again?" it read.

Probably not, Jolie thought. She was leaving. Rebecca Grolund was already part of her past.

Jolie shivered and pulled the institution surplus blankets up around her shoulders. The spartan room might have seemed nicer if it hadn't turned into a prison. Sitting on the bed cross-legged, Jolie could see the sun rising over the buildings across the street, the frozen dew making their roofs glisten like some crazy fairy had dumped all her dust on them.

This is it; Solstice. The shortest day of the year, she thought. If Mem had been alive, people would be hurrying in and out of the big old house to see what they could do to help, bringing dishes of food, setting up tables with white linen tablecloths, and huge vases full of flowers. By evening, the house would smell like cinnamon, oranges, and Cajun spices, filled with happy people held together by the soft jazz floating from room to room. Great Aunt Jessamin and Grandpere Blancflor always "dropped by" claiming they couldn't stay, then stayed until dawn. Attending the pagan celebration was a big concession for the Catholic Blancflors, but in truth, Jolie never saw them happier. Their daughter Tessa, "the beautiful" would be there, surrounded by a circle of admiring men, her long dark hair shining like she'd brushed in moonbeams.

Topi, the man Jolie had thought would become her father, would be there too; Topi, who had come to the Solstice party one year and never left: a member of the family from that first night.

Back then Jolie thought the whole world came to Mem's for Solstice, and even after eleven years, the memories were so strong, all she had to do was close her eyes, and she was there again, walking the familiar rooms. Everything looked as it had, except Mem was not there.

Jolie's childhood world had been an extended family of several dozen, plus a hundred or so of her grandmother's closest friends. And though she'd lived in many places since, and seen lots of things, her life had never felt as rich as it had among her family in New Orleans. For years, the only stability she and Jessie had was each other. That would change when Jolie left. She would only have herself to look after or rely on.

Footsteps approached the door. A key rattled in the lock and Father Owen stepped in.

"Good morning, Miss Figg. How are you this morning?"

Jolie noted his use of her last name. He had been talking to someone.

"I'm pissed. I came to you for help and you locked me up like a prisoner."

"I'm sorry. I was afraid if I didn't, you might do something foolish."

"Or that I already had?"

Chapter Twelve

Father Owen smiled apologetically. "You'll be relieved to know there was no ax murder at Mae McBride's last night. However, her mother-in-law was quite alarmed when you banged on the window. News is good, though, they expect her to be released from the hospital this morning."

"The hospital?" Jolie got to her feet. "If Faith's all right, why is she in the hospital?"

"They aren't sure, but they think she may have had a small stroke or heart attack."

"You don't find that a strange coincidence, Father Owen; Faith having to go to the hospital with some mysterious symptom and the black fog covering her house?"

"No. I do not. Fog may be rare here in the Southwest but it's not unknown. What you saw might have been someone's sprinklers coming on, or the mist from a neighbor's misters floating over from a nearby yard."

"It's December. No one is running misters."

"When we are frightened in the dark, who can tell what we see, and what we turn it into? I've found most 'occult' events turn out to be explainable without getting into anything magical. Faith's attack was caused by a frightened girl banging on her window in the middle of the night"

"Great."

"Faith made it clear she did not blame you in any way. Mae, however, is another story. I would steer clear of the McBride's for awhile."

"So now what?"

"Now, I think it is time to call your mother."

Jolie set her jaw. "You can't send me back there."

"You're too young to see it this way now, but this is for your own good. Running away is a dangerous business."

"Sometimes staying is worse," Jolie's voice cracked.

"Then tell me what happened, and let me get you help."

"You mean call CPS or Juvenile Probation? No thanks."

"If someone has hurt you, they need to be stopped. You may be strong enough to get past this, but there will be others who are not."

"It's not like that." Jolie knew it was a half truth. It wasn't like that--yet, and she had left so that it wouldn't be. Jolie's body clenched like a fist, but she didn't need to be a psychic to see the outcome of this conversation. She was either going to Child Haven or back to the trailer park. She picked up her backpack and slung her jacket over her shoulder.

"She won't be up yet. It's only seven. She's still sleeping."

"Then we'll wake her up. Come on."

Jolie followed Father Owen back to his office, pulled out her cell phone, and gave him Jesse's number. The voicemail picked up and he left a brief message.

Jolie gave him a tight smile. "Guess you're stuck with me for a little while longer."

"That's okay. How about breakfast?" Father Owen led her to a small kitchenette that looked out over the garden, pulled out a chair, and indicated she should sit down. The multi-colored dotted linoleum floor was older than Jolie's parents, and the cupboard doors wouldn't close anymore because of all the layers of paint, but the thorny garden outside was flooded with sunshine and a pot of tea had already been set to brewing.

Chapter Twelve

"What would you like?" Father Owen opened the small cupboard. "Cold cereal? We have Cheerios and Cheerios. We also have toaster waffles, compliments of some of the congregation who love Costco, or orange juice, toast, and eggs.

"Can I have both? I'm pretty hungry."

"Me too. Why don't you help yourself to cereal while I try not to burn the eggs?"

"Okay."

Father Owen set to cooking while Jolie downed a quick bowl of Cheerios and poured small glasses of OJ for them both.

"So are you ever going to talk to me about what happened last night?" Father Owen asked as he set the eggs on the table, "the real story, not the 'I can make something up for this old fart' version."

"Cut the sugar coating and give you the bad stuff, is that it?"

"Unless you want to tell me about the pony your folks got you for your last birthday and how much they adore you. It would be refreshing to hear that. I don't hear much from happy families. People mostly turn to God, and priests, when things aren't going well."

"You won't believe me."

"There must be some part that doesn't involve magic for its veracity? How about the men you said were chasing you, let's start there."

Jolie squinted against the sunshine streaming in the window. What could she say that would make any difference? Telling Father Owen about Rick wouldn't change anything. Chasing a runaway wasn't a crime. Rick would be back on their doorstep before the day was out and she'd be in more trouble than ever. And Sean? She didn't know what to think about Sean, but she didn't want to get him in trouble.

"Why'd you run away?" Father Owen prodded.

"I was pissed and tired of feeling like my house wasn't my house. Look, what's the big deal? I'm almost sixteen. Why do I have to live with my mom? She's never there and when she is, she's partying with her boyfriends. I'm the responsible one. I'm the grown up. I get myself off to school, I make sure I have lunch money, I cook dinner, do the laundry, clean the trailer, and keep my grades up. I do all of that--not her. So why can't I just live on my own? Things would be so much easier."

"Kids who run away always think that, but too often they find out they're wrong. Some end up dead wrong. You seem like a bright girl, Jolie. You want to be a grown up? Finish school, get a diploma, then a job. Learn from your parent's mistakes and make the life you want for yourself."

"But that's what I'm trying to do. That's why I had to leave. All of this stuff with Mom just keeps pulling me down."

"What about your father? Couldn't you go stay with him?"

"I don't think so. He's dead."

"I'm sorry." Father Owen waited for Jolie to say something more. She didn't. "Is there someone else, some other family that might take you in?"

"I don't know." *There was once,* she thought. "They were in New Orleans." Mem would have taken her in a minute, but would any of the rest of the family? She'd been a little girl when Jessie took her away. Now she was a teenager with issues--a stranger they didn't even know. She began to reconsider her welcome in New Orleans. They might not want her. "They have their own lives, though, you know? Why would they want to take on another kid?"

Chapter Twelve

Father Owen sighed. "Jolie, you're going to have to start trusting someone sometime, because, believe it or not, that's what grownups do. They trust that the guy in the other car is going to stay in his lane. They trust their kids are being taught something when they go to school. They trust their employers are going to give them their paychecks and it just goes on and on. It's not perfect, but without basic trust, nothing good happens. So I want you to ask yourself, who can you trust?"

Jolie put down her spoon and sat back in her chair. "I trusted Faith McBride. That's why I banged on her window."

CHAPTER THIRTEEN

Jessie Lynn was waiting for Jolie and Father Owen in the church's foyer. She looked as if she'd been tossed out of a semi and driven over a few times. Dark circles ringed her eyes, one a lot darker than the other. Jolie's resolve to let Jessie Lynn take care of herself vanished like hair mousse between her fingers.

"Are you all right, Mom?" She eyed the bruise on Jessie's face.

Jessie Lynn nodded. "Are you?"

"Yeah. Look, I'm sorry. I just couldn't stay there anymore."

"I know, but Rick's gone, Jolie. I swear. I threw him out." After a pause she added, "And he'll stay gone, I promise."

Father Owen waited silently for the twisted glue that holds families together to work... or not.

Jessie turned to him. "Thank you, Father. Do I owe you something, for food or something?"

"Of course not. This is what we're here for."

"So I can take her home?"

"That's where she belongs, don't you think,? She's a strong, young lady, Ms. Figg. You should be proud."

"I am." Jessie's chin went up, defensively.

"You were lucky this time--both of you. A case worker would have asked about influences in the home." He glanced at Jessie Lynn's black eye. "Violence, drugs, alcohol."

Jessie's hand shook as she put dark sunglasses on over her black eyes.

"Jolie doesn't do drugs," she muttered.

Chapter Thirteen

"I wasn't talking about Jolie. People that visit your home have an influence on your daughter, too, good or bad, and as the adult, you're the one expected to be responsible, and decide who is acceptable, and who is not."

"Look, you did us a favor, Father, I understand that, but you don't know anything about our lives." Jessie glared at Jolie, her eyes accusing her daughter of having said things she should not have.

"I'm sorry. You're right of course. I didn't mean to offend you, Ms. Figg. I just see so many single mothers struggling to find a balance between their needs and the demands of being a parent. Jolie is getting older, she's almost an adult, but she's still in your care for a few more years, so right now, you're making choices for both of you, and if you make a mistake, she's the one likely to suffer the most."

Jessie Lynn looked like she would either burst into tears or scratch the priest's eyes out; the balance was tipping back and forth. Jolie rolled her eyes and made a grimace at Father Owen

"Thanks, Father. I'll take it from here." She put an arm around her mom's shoulders and led Jessie out to the truck.

Driving back into the trailer park felt like chewing on freeze dried failure.

This was why they'd moved so many times--this feeling of walking through a battlefield surrounded by the unburied cadavers of your hopes and dreams. Staring at their dead eyes and knowing with terrible certainty that they would never rise again. Jessie Lynn had never been able to handle this feeling. Her answer was to pack up and move on, hoping that next time, in a new place, a new town, a new state, it would somehow, magically be different.

Jolie knew the pattern well.

"I'd like to stay through the end of the school year," she said quietly.

"It won't be easy. Rick's not good at taking 'no'. We can change the locks but maybe it would be better to find another place--maybe an apartment this time, huh? What do you think?" she tried to force cheerfulness into her voice, but it wasn't working. Jolie avoided saying that as long as Jessie worked at the same bar, Rick would have no problem finding them, no matter where they moved. She didn't have to. They'd been through the scenario before. If the ex-boyfriend accepted the breakup, things went easier. If he didn't, all they could do was disappear.

"I don't care where we live, Mom, as long as it's in the same school zone, okay?"

"You like it there, baby? You're doing all right?"

No. It sucks! Jolie wanted to shout. But changing schools had never made anything better. "I just can't afford to lose any more credits," she opted for the half truth.

"Okay." Jessie Lynn nodded. "I'll look around." But Jolie knew Jessie had already decided Las Vegas was not their "someplace." She would start looking for an apartment, then one day, she'd come home with a roadmap.

"So and so said there were jobs in Timbuktu. I thought we should check it out. I have an interview next week."

I'm never going to graduate. Jolie glanced over at her mom. Jolie wasn't the only one getting older. Jessie Lynn Figg was thirty-five and looked ten years older. How many more times would she be able to search for her someplace? She had nothing, no resources, no skills: nothing, except Jolie.

Chapter Thirteen

Jolie rolled down the window and looked up at the winter sky. In a few hours, it would be dark.

"It's Solstice," she said, letting the cold air brighten her cheeks. "Remember Mem's big parties?"

"Yeah," Jessie answered, tight-lipped. "You remember that? You were so little."

"I remember. They were the best." She paused. "Mom, why did we leave New Orleans, really? The big girl answer this time."

The truck's headlights swept the trailer as Jessie Lynn pulled in. She stopped it and sat, not moving.

"There was nothing for us there. Your father and I weren't married. They didn't care about us."

"Mem did."

"Mem was old. She was losing it. Whatever influence she had, was going with her mind." Jessie opened her door.

"But the family..." Jolie began to protest. Jessie stopped her.

"They're not our family," Jessie spat back. "They were going to take you away from me. Do you understand? They said I wasn't a fit mother and I shouldn't be allowed to raise you--my own child." Jessie got out of the truck, slamming the door behind her. She stomped up to the trailer.

They tried to keep me. The thought loosened the tight knot inside Jolie. *They didn't just let me go. They tried to keep me with them. The news was strangely comforting.*

Jolie got out of the truck and followed her mother inside, hovering in the doorway. Jessie had turned on a light and was staring out the window over the sink as if seeing something far away.

"You were just a kid, Jo. You didn't see things the way I did." She sighed, wearily. "And you're a good person. You always believe the best in people—unless, of course, they want to date me." She turned and gave her daughter a wry smile.

The tension between them thawed. These were the good times; when it was just the two of them and Jessie was sober. The bond between them might not always be a healthy one, but it was strong.

Jolie walked through the trailer to her room, looking around at all the stuff she had thought she'd never see again. She wouldn't have missed any of it. But here she was and here it was: weird.

Jessie was wrong. Jolie had seen things. She had seen how Jessie and Topi had been happy together until Jessie had started drinking again. She'd seen how they fought, not with words or fists but silently, coldly, pulling into themselves, Jessie had punished Topi by hurting herself. Topi had punished Jessie by treating her with gentle kindness right up until the day he insisted Jessie stop destroying herself, and think about Jolie and her future. Jessie had packed their things and left in the middle of the night without another word.

Jolie turned at the door to her bedroom. "Why'd you walk out on him? Topi was the best thing that ever happened to us." Jolie watched her mom's face, knowing this was dangerous territory.

"I didn't walk out, he--forget it, Jolie. You wouldn't understand. He was always so careful not to argue in front of you. He was crazy about you. I think that's why he stayed as long as he did. It sure as hell wasn't because he loved me."

"He loved you, Mom. I know he did." She paused. "So, does he still live in New Orleans?"

Jessie's jaw tensed. "Nobody lives in New Orleans anymore, honey"

Chapter Thirteen

Jolie was sure it wasn't true. Jessie knew exactly where Topi was--or had been until Katrina scattered most of New Orleans over the Southern states. "Topi would go back. He'd never leave. Hey, I know, why don't we take a trip when school gets out? We could go..."

"No," Jessie cut her off. "Look, Jolie, every time I go through a breakup, you start in about Topi and New Orleans. Stop thinking like a little kid with your happily ever after shit. Topi and I are never getting back together."

"But he loves you, Mom. I know he does."

"You don't know anything."

"Mom..."

Jessie spun around. "He's married, Jolie." Tears glittered in her eyes.

Married? How could that be? Topi couldn't just marry some stranger. They were a family. In the dream they all said they would be there--they promised they would be together.

"Maybe they got divorced," Jolie said, hesitantly. "Maybe it didn't work out..."

"God, don't you ever quit? You're so quick to judge every other guy who screws me over, but when it comes to Topi you have this amazing blind spot. The truth is, Topi was just like your dad and all the others, he used us, then threw us away."

Jolie shook her head. "That's not fair. Dad died. He couldn't help that."

"All those gifted people and none of them could have warned him not to go to Nicaragua to help those people? I told him, and I'm no psychic. Fakes; that's all those Boulets' are fakes. They don't have special powers. They don't have special anything." Jolie knew better than to get into this argument.

"Topi would never want to hurt you, Mom. How do you know he doesn't regret what happened just as much as you do, and wish he could change it?"

"Because he married Tessa, okay? That's how."

Jolie was stunned. *Tessa? Tessa the beautiful? Tessa of the long dark hair?*

"Yeah, that Tessa. Surprised? You shouldn't be. She got it all, the gifts, Mem's little secrets, and Topi. The only thing she didn't get was you, and Mem was the last one standing in the way of that. She was always telling them to leave us alone, that we needed to be together, but her mind was going. Everyone could see it. She didn't have much time left and once she was gone, there'd be no one left to stand up for us. So I took you and went." Jessie Lynn fumbled for a cigarette and a lighter. "I should have left you there. You would have been fine--you would have been happy, but I needed someone, you know?" She sniffled and wiped her eyes. "I'm sorry your mom is such a fuck up." Her thin shoulders drooped as she sucked in the smoke, then let it out.

"It's okay. We'll get through this, Mom. We always do."

"Yeah, right. We're doing great," her voice dripped with sarcasm.

Jolie walked back to her room, threw her backpack in a corner, and lay down on the bed. In the other room, Jessie turned on the TV. After a few minutes Jolie got up and drifted through the living room, but she didn't feel like watching anything. Her brain was in overdrive. She grabbed her jacket.

"Don't go anywhere. You're grounded," Jessie said as Jolie went out the door.

Jolie sat on the front steps, watching the sky darken, waiting for the longest night of the year to begin in

Chapter Thirteen

earnest. The homeless woman came around the corner and sat down beside her, wrapped in a new, old blanket.

"When you left last night, I thought you were gone for good."

Jolie shrugged. "It didn't work out."

"Life's like that more than not. I'm glad you're back, though. When I saw your mom driving in with you tonight, it made me feel safer."

Jolie raised one eyebrow. "That just proves how crazy you are." They both smiled. In the silence that followed, it was understood that they had become friends. "I don't even know your name," Jolie said quietly.

It's not important." The old woman hesitated. "But you can call me Betty."

"That's your name? Betty?"

"It's what people call me."

Jolie thought about that. "You know, Betty, I was thinking about what you said before, about your teeth and how it's like there's little radios playing in them. Is that really what happens?"

"How would I know? I'm crazy."

"Right. But see, I read this story on the internet and it said that fifteen years ago some people got these new fillings and then started hearing the radio all the time-- just out of nowhere, and no one knew why."

"So what did they do, these people?" the old woman asked.

"Somebody finally believed them enough to do some tests."

"And...?"

"They took out the fillings and the radio stuff stopped."

"And they weren't crazy anymore?"

"No crazier than they were before, I guess."

E.F. Winters

The woman clutched the blanket, looking down the lane between the trailers.

"You okay?" Jolie asked.

"I was just thinking about my old life. I don't even know if it's there anymore, or if it would be possible to go back now."

"You'll never know unless you try. When I ran away, I didn't think anybody would miss me."

"And you were wrong."

"Maybe you are too," Jolie said. "Maybe they miss you every day and wish they could see you again. I know that's how I feel about my grandmother."

"Where is she?"

"In heaven I guess. So I can't ever get my wish, but maybe there's some other kid who could get theirs."

"They probably think I'm dead after all this time."

"It'd be fun to see the look on their faces when they found out you weren't though, wouldn't it?"

"Yeah." The old woman shuffled her feet in the dirt. "They said I was crazy. They were going to move me out of my house, and lock me up in a hospital."

"Your kids?"

"Yeah."

"They didn't know what was going on. They probably just wanted to keep you safe until you could get well, but if the radio stopped, it would be different, wouldn't it?"

The old woman's face had the wistfulness of a child, then suddenly, her eyes clouded. "This is Sky View traffic…" She stood and began to walk down the lane.

Jolie watched her, then got up, and went back inside.

Jessie Lynn was putting on her coat.

"What's up? I thought you had the night off?"

Chapter Thirteen

"Somebody called in." Jessie threw her daughter a sheepish look. "I know, it stinks, but we aren't doing anything anymore, right? And if we have to move, we'll need the money. Don't wait up. I'll be late."

CHAPTER FOURTEEN

Cleaning up the trailer was an act of defiance, as if by throwing away old beer bottles and emptying ashtrays, she could reclaim her space and wipe away Rick's existence. Jolie put on rubber gloves, found a package of incense, and lit a stick. She didn't even want the smell of his leftover fast food hanging around.

She was wiping down the dinette cushions when she saw a bump like something had been stuck down behind them. Hoping she wasn't about to be grossed out, she wriggled her gloved fingers down until she grasped an edge and pulled it out. It was Jessie Lynn's old address book; the one Jolie had thought was lost in the bottom of a box in the shed. When had Jessie brought it in? Why had she? Had she called New Orleans when she found out Jolie was missing? Had she gotten hold of anyone?

The book's leather jacket was soft and floppy, its edges tattered. A faded mandala had been stamped into the leather and the green dye, worn from the smooth places, had settled into the grooves of the design. Jolie began to turn the pages, looking at the numbers and addresses; Anderson, Appleton, Bourgain... What part of her history did these names hold? Who were these people to Jessie--and therefore to Jolie? Whatever Jessie remembered about her birth parents and family, she had never shared. The series of nameless foster families that followed were barely a side note in her mother's story. It was as if Jessie Lynn Figg's story had begun when she met Lucien Boulet.

Jolie continued to thumb through the entries. Many had been erased, their shadows ghosting on the page.

Chapter Fourteen

Some had notations like "not good number" or "letter returned" written by them and a single line drawn through. Others had been scribbled through until they were obliterated as if this would remove the person permanently from Jessie's life.

Jolie held the book under the dinette's light, peering at the yellowing pages, trying to match names to vaguely remembered faces; a picnic, a camping trip, a day at the lake. An old black and white photograph of a middle-aged man with a big fish, its white border cut out into decorative ripples, fluttered to the floor. The date stamped on the border was 1962 but there was no name or any writing to give any clue as to why Jessie had saved it. Jolie examined the man's eyes, nose, mouth. Were any of them like her mother's or hers? Was the man with the fish a Figg, or just some foster dad that deserved to be remembered?

Jolie turned another page. Aunt Jessamin's name was written at the top in fine, educated letters. This was not Jessie Lynn's immature scrawl. Someone else had made this entry. Jolie stared at the number. Below it, a violent scribble had almost completely blocked out the next name but it began with a "T".

Tessa, Jolie thought. This had been cousin Tessa's number. Was it still? Was Topi there with her now? Did the family still carry on Mem's tradition? If they did, they would all be together tonight.

It's a fantasy. It doesn't exist, Jessie had said. But Jolie always gave in to her mother, that was how they'd gotten into this mess. Jolie picked up the phone, held it to her ear, then put it back down and went back to cleaning. Calling New Orleans now felt like betrayal.

She finished cleaning, drew a deep breath, and looked around. The Christmas lights came on at the trailer next door.

E.F. Winters

It's Solstice proper now, Jolie thought, sadly. *The most sacred night of the year for thousands of years.* The trailer suddenly felt cramped and lonely, and she wished her mother hadn't gone to work. Maybe they could have gone to see Faith in the hospital. But Faith wouldn't be at the hospital, would she? She'd be at the Solstice celebration with the others.

Jolie looked out the window and felt a shiver climb her spine. Pulling off her jeans she put on an oversized tee shirt, foraged until she found a half-empty bag of chips and a soda. She crawled onto her mom's bed and turned on the TV.

The Nightmare Before Christmas was on. She scrolled to another channel. She could watch the billionth re-run of Rudolph the Red-Nosed Reindeer, complete with extra snow, courtesy of the static of poor reception. The third local station they didn't get was total fuzz. She switched back to The Nightmare Before Christmas.

Pathetic, she thought. "It's Solstice and the best I can do is stale chips, a soda, and Jack Pumpkin Head. I love the holidays."

Jolie sat in front of the movie. Her eyes wandered over to the address book. She watched the movie, but her eyes kept tracking back. Suddenly, in one explosive leap, she launched from the bed, ran up the center aisle, and picked up the phone. Opening up to Jessamin's listing, she punched in the number before she could talk herself out of it. It was a holiday. What was more natural than calling family on a holiday when she was all alone and didn't have anyone else to talk to?

She waited nervously while the phone on the other end rang.

No one answered. When the generic recorded message came on, she slammed the receiver down. In the

Chapter Fourteen

birthing dream, they were all there, encouraging her, and promising they would be there to help. She had believed for years that they had broken this promise, but as torn as she would have been at five, to be separated from Jessie, knowing the Boulets had tried to keep her, had changed everything. Biting her lip, Jolie stared at the scribble that hid Tessa's number. Above it was written "Mem" and the number eight, in firm square lettering. Using the side of a pencil, Jolie turned to the next page in the phone book, lightly shading over it to expose the indent from the previous page. It was a trick she'd seen in old detective movies. The indent the pen had left could often be seen on the page beneath it once it had been shaded. But of course, the scribbles were there too. Jessie Lynn had pressed hard when she tried to scratch Tessa from her life. Jolie peered at the page. The page went blank and she saw the numbers being written on the page fresh in flowing fluid script.

"Here, I'll just write Tessa's number in here for you as well, in case you need it." It was Jessamin's soft, lilting drawl. *"Mem's is the same only with an eight at the end. That'll be easy for you to remember."*

Jolie bit her lip and began to punch in the area code and number.

It rang and rang, but no voice came on to say it was disconnected. Would they have given the number back out to someone else by now? Could they do that? Mem had the number for years and years. Crap, half the parish had it posted on their fridge.

Jolie was about to hang up when someone picked up.

"Hello?" the person on the other end said, shouting over party background noise.

"Topi?" Strains of jazz, laughter, and conversation trickled through the phone's earpiece. "Topi, it's me,

E.F. Winters

Jolie." Jolie felt ridiculously happy, awkward, and stupid at the same time.

"What? What did you say, love? I'm sorry I can't hear very well. The music is very big."

"I said it's me, Topi. It's Jolie!"

"Jolie? Jolie! Oh my God, I can't believe it. Jolie. Is it really you? Where are you?"

"I'm in Las Vegas. We're living in Las Vegas now." Tears ran down Jolie's cheeks.

"You are in Las Vegas, you say?" He seemed to be having a hard time comprehending that. "Are you all right?"

"Yeah, I'm fine. We're both fine." She sniffled and wiped her face with her tee shirt.

"Really, you are fine," he repeated with such a sense of relief that Jolie could feel it all the way across the country. "Everyone will be so happy to hear it."

"Is everyone there? Aunt Jessamin, and Grandpere... Tessa?"

"Yes, yes, we are all here, everyone, except you and Jessie, and Mem of course." He hesitated. "How is Jessie?"

Jolie didn't know what to say. How did you tell your mom's old flame that she'd never recovered from their break up?

"She's at work," Jolie dodged the question.

"Oh, that's good, she's at work. So you are alone, tonight then, on Solstice?"

There was a long silence.

"Yes." There was another silence during which Jolie thought she heard Topi sniffling and whispering to someone in the background.

"I'm so sorry. It's wrong. You should not be alone. You should be with us," he muttered.

Chapter Fourteen

"I've been thinking maybe I could come for a visit this summer?" she said cautiously. "If you think it would be okay?"

"Yes, of course, of course--a visit. A visit would be more than okay," Topi said happily. "We would love to have you for a visit anytime."

For a visit. The words wrung her heart. A small female voice rose from the background noise and Jolie could hear Topi mumbling something. "Tell your mama, Zu-zu. I'll be right there. Daddy's talking on the phone right now, baby."

"What? What was that? I couldn't hear you," Jolie said.

"I'm sorry, that was Zu-zu, our little girl--Tessa and mine; your little cousin." Topi laughed.

Jolie felt like a swarm of killer bees were stinging her heart. Topi had another little girl. She had been replaced.

Don't be an idiot, she told herself. *What did you think was going to happen--that everything was going to stay frozen in time there while you went away?*

"So, you have children?" she managed to say, hoping to hide her disappointment. "That's great."

"Yes, we have two boys, Zeke and Yuri, and then Zu-Zu is our youngest. They are beautiful children, Jolie. Very special--like you. I cannot wait for you to meet them, and for them to meet you." There was another silence. "Everyone has worried about you. We miss you so very much, but you really are okay?"

Jolie could hardly speak around the lump in her throat. "Yeah. I'm fine. I miss you all too," she muttered. She didn't want him to hear her cry. She didn't want him to know she was miserable and felt like there was a big hole in her side, and she had thought about them every day since Jessie had taken her away.

"Hey, I have to go now, Topi. Some friends are picking me up to go to a party," she lied. "I just wanted to say hello, and wish everybody happy Solstice."

"I'm so glad you did," Topi's voice melted over her like caramel syrup; all buttery and sweet. "You will call again soon, won't you? And make plans for coming? You have given us all a wonderful gift--to know you are all right and doing well. You are always in our thoughts and prayers, Joliette."

"Sure. I'm sorry. I really do have to go."

"Wait. Give me your number so we can call you."

"No, you shouldn't call here. I don't think mom would-- Please, don't. I'll call again. I promise. I gotta go. Happy Solstice." Jolie hung up. Sobbing, she threw herself onto the bed and cried herself to sleep.

It was the rumble of a truck engine that woke her. The Nightmare Before Christmas was over and Nightmare on Elm Street had started. *Stupid programming*, Jolie thought, groggily looking at the clock by Jessie's bed. It was seven--too early for her mom to be home. A car door slammed outside. *Somebody must be visiting the neighbors*, she told herself, trying to calm the feeling of dread creeping through her, as the sound of heavy boots came toward the trailer.

Jolie stared at the door. Everything moved in slow motion as the mechanism in the door handle moved. Why hadn't they changed the locks? That there hadn't been time, seemed like a lame excuse right now. Jessie had gone to work, leaving Jolie home alone, and Rick still had a key. The metal parts fell into place and the door opened.

Jolie's eyes seemed to be the only part of her that was not frozen. Frantically flitting around the trailer, they searched for a way to disappear, but single wide

Chapter Fourteen

trailers did not come with hiding places. There was no place Rick couldn't get to with a simple kick.

"Time to go, girls. Are you ready?" Rick called out. He saw Jolie. "Hey kid, where's your mom?"

"At work."

"At work?" he frowned.

"I guess she figured since you two broke up, the Solstice thing was off."

"Broke up? Where'd you get a crazy idea like that? We didn't break up. It was just a little tiff." Rick's attitude dared her to challenge the statement. "I'm not going anywhere." His smile was not friendly.

"Man, and I already washed my hair to celebrate," Jolie said, sarcastically. It was a mangled version of a line from some old movie, a feeble attempt to show him she wasn't scared.

"Well then, I guess she's just going to miss all the fun." Rick went into Jolie's room and came out with a pair of her jeans. "Get dressed, smart mouth." He tossed them at her. "We've got a long drive."

"I can't. I'm grounded," Jolie lied. "Mom told me I wasn't allowed to go anywhere."

Rick put his face in hers. "Put on your pants or I'll do it for you."

Jolie glared and he glared back, but he was stone cold sober, and dead serious. Jolie took the jeans and began slipping them on under her oversized tee shirt, keenly aware of how little she had on, and how vulnerable she was. "Where are we going?" She tried to distract him by talking.

"To the Solstice Ceremony, remember?" Rick answered. "We're expected."

Wrapped in her old army surplus jacket, Jolie followed Rick out into the cold, walking as if she was on her way to face a firing squad. This whole thing felt like a very bad idea. As she neared the pickup, Jolie suddenly veered and tried to make a break for it. Rick's tattooed arm circled her waist, lifting her off her feet.

"Where do you think you're going?"

"Let me go. I don't want to do this, Rick. I'm not going." Her feet flailed above the ground.

"The hell you aren't. You're not making me look bad in front of my friends." He tried to open the truck's door and still keep hold of her while she struggled to get free.

"You can't make me when I don't want to. Faith won't allow it."

"Faith won't even be there. She's in the hospital, but then you know all about that, don't you? You're going and you're going to behave." He tried to stuff her into the truck.

"I'm not!" she fought back.

"Leave her alone," the homeless woman's voice was shaky but the look in her eyes was steady. "She said she didn't want to go with you."

"Get out of here, old woman. This is none of your business." Rick pushed Betty away, trying to close Jolie into the pickup.

"Jolie, get out of the truck," Betty shouted, pulling on Rick's arm.

"I told you to mind your own business, old woman!" Rick turned on the Betty, lifting one arm, his fist balled, ready to punch her.

"No, Rick don't!" Jolie grabbed his arm. Instantly the vision she'd seen before, where the old woman got beaten to death began--this time from Rick's point of view. She felt like she was going to vomit. "Stop, Rick. Stop, both of you." Jolie fixed her eyes on the old woman. "I'm going. Okay, I'm going. I'll be fine, Betty. Just step back. Please, leave this be. I don't want you to

Chapter Fourteen

get hurt." Jolie got in the truck. "See, I'm in. Let's go." She slammed the door shut. Rick let go of Betty and lowered his fist.

"Stay out of other people's business. You'll live longer," he grumbled getting into the truck.

Rick's El Camino topped a hill. Its headlights shone on a long straight stretch of Highway 95 that dipped down to a desert valley as flat as a floor then disappeared into the unlit night. To the southwest, shadowy mountains rose in the distance, a jagged line of black against the moonless sky. To the east, Jolie could see the lights of Boulder City. To the west, a distant string of headlights marked I-15 running south to Los Angeles.

For the first twenty miles, there was only the El Camino and a loose string of semi-trucks on the road. Jolie took out her phone and began to text Jessie. She probably wouldn't get it until too late to do anything, but there was always a chance.

"What are you doing?"

"Texting Mom that I'm with you so she won't be worried."

Rick did not comment. The text would not send.

"Shit," Jolie swore under her breath. She was on her own.

After they took the turnoff marked "Nelson", even the commercial truck traffic was gone. As far as Jolie could see, there was only dark empty desert.

"Where is this place? Looks like we're going to a rattlesnake roundup," she commented.

"We aren't lookin' for tourists."

"Is it somebody's ranch or something?"

"Nope."

"What if I have to pee?"

"There's a port-a-potty."

"Gross."

"Then you can hold it--like you'll hold your tongue if you know what's good for you. I am not going to be embarrassed by you."

They turned off the paved road onto a dirt road that ran back toward the South and East. Jolie tried to keep her bearings, looking for any kind of marker in the terrain in case she had to find her own way back home.

If the road kept on in this direction it would run right into the trickle people still called the Colorado River. As long as you could see the distant glow above the brightest spot on Earth, it was pretty hard to get lost anywhere near Las Vegas. The El Camino bumped over washboards in the road, dips, and shallow ruts. The road was passable without four-wheel drive, but no one would have called it "good," and Jolie had a hard time imagining people like the coven ladies, driving their clean little city sedans out here.

Lights up ahead told her they were nearing their destination. She rolled down the window.

"Shut that, it's freezing out there."

"Sorry. I farted," Jolie lied, knowing that would shut him up.

She could see cars and hear voices up ahead now. Sparks were flying into the night sky from a big bonfire beyond an embankment, and she could see the silhouettes of people's heads moving by it.

While Rick parked, Jolie checked out the parking lot. Sean's motorcycle was not far away. He had come after all. She smiled in spite of herself. There were a few other bikes, a few SUVs, and some smaller compacts, but mostly people had come in vans and pickups. An older model Chevy that looked like one that had been parked at Mae's looked familiar. She didn't have a great feeling about the night's activities, but it was reassuring to know there were going to be other people around. The

Chapter Fourteen

darkest ceremonies happened in small groups where secrets could be controlled. Most of the pseudo-witches Jolie had met through her mother had no idea what they were doing. They were just making it up as they went along, and that made them both naive and dangerous.

Hanging back so people wouldn't think they were together, Jolie followed Rick around the end of the hill encircling the ceremonial area.

Rory sat on a folding chair near the fire, holding court. A silent portable CD player sat on the ground nearby, and a dozen participants milled around, apparently waiting for a word with him.

Jolie caught the flash of a bright red head on the far side of the fire, and for a minute wondered if it was Tru. There were way more people here than just the coven ladies and Rick's crew. So if Faith was in the hospital and wasn't coming, who was doing the ceremony? She looked over at Rory, sitting all smug and important. That was it. That was the plan. With Faith out of the way, Rory was in charge of the ceremony. *This is not good.* Jolie heard a boisterous, unselfconscious laugh and turned to see Sean talking to a bunch of biker chicks. He looked up and saw Rick, then Jolie, but whatever he was thinking, he was keeping it to himself.

Rick pushed Jolie toward a group of women gathered around an RV.

"Mae and her blue hairs are over there. They'll tell you what to do."

As Jolie walked toward the RV, Sean broke off from his friends and moved to intercept her.

"Are you all right?" he asked, falling into step beside her.

"No thanks to you."

"Me? What did I do?"

"You could answer that better than I could."

E.F. Winters

Jolie kept walking until the crowd around the RV swallowed her. It was territory few heterosexual males would brave.

CHAPTER FIFTEEN

"**W**ell, aren't you full of surprises?" Tru planted herself in Jolie's path wearing a grin as wide as a ten-year-old at her birthday party. "I never figured on running into you again, and sure as hell not here."

"Hey, Tru. Is Marty here too?" Jolie was surprised at how relieved she was to see a familiar face and even more surprised that she felt that way about Tru; someone she barely knew.

"Where I go, Marty goes." Tru smiled with shy pride.

"That's great. I wouldn't have thought he was the type to go for this kind of stuff."

"Oh God no, he absolutely is not." Tru laughed. "Angels save me from 'the type'. No, Marty is big, simple, and as sweet as they come. He's got no interest in snake tattoos, or piercing his privates, or any of that if you know what I mean?"

"Yeah, I kinda do," Jolie admitted. Tru, she decided, was a fringer; someone who had a passing acquaintance with Wicca because she was drawn to its romantic side. She might dip her toes in the water but she wouldn't dive in and swim. Tonight that could be a good thing.

"Marty's interests in magic begin and end with Dungeons and Dragons. He just comes along with me when I want to go, you know, so he can protect me."

"From what?"

Tru laughed. "Beats me."

Marty had come just to be with Tru because he loved her. He might not be the hunkiest guy in the world but he would stand by her whatever she did. Jolie felt a twinge of envy. Would someone ever be willing to put up with her crazy world and do that for her?

She looked out over the growing crowd. Rory's dark groupies glared with malevolent eyes, shrouded in smudged kohl, at the airy fairies and the middle of the road fringers swelling the ranks.

Wannabees... Sheep... There are so many people... I hope it isn't weird this year... If they only knew... Jolie picked up bits and pieces as she scanned the crowd.

"Maybe tonight you should keep Marty close, just to be safe," she said quietly.

"Why?" Tru frowned. "Is something wrong?"

Before Jolie could answer, Mae McBride appeared at her elbow, dressed in the kind of loose flowy dress worn by older women with expanding middles and disposable incomes, who made a hobby of enlightenment. She looked at Jolie as if she were a bug crawling across her spotless dining room table.

"I can't believe you had the nerve to show up after last night, Miss Figg." Her thin lips looked like a thread had been sewn through them, then pulled tight.

"It wasn't my idea. Hey, if you've got someone else, that's fine by me. Just tell Rick that I'm out, so I can go home."

"Oh, you're the virgin!" Tru shrieked. Everyone within a square mile stopped to stare. "That's great, Jolie!" Just to make sure everyone knew exactly who Tru meant, she put an arm around Jolie's shoulders and gave her a squeeze. Jolie shrugged out of the embrace.

"Maybe not. Like I said, none of this was my idea."

Whatever Mae was about to say was trumped by Mickey's head poking out of the RV door.

"There you are, Jolie. Thank heaven. We were beginning to think you wouldn't make it. Go play girls. Find me in the circle when its time for the ceremony."

Chapter Fifteen

Mickey stepped aside, revealing two miniature versions of herself. "My big girls," she bragged with a smile.

"They look...sweet," Jolie said, aware she was expected to say something nice about Mickey's progeny, but unsure of the etiquette. "How many kids do you have?"

"Four. All Girls." Mickey sighed. "Hey, Tru," she greeted the redhead.

"Hey, Mickey."

"You know each other?"

"Boulder's a small town, Jolie, especially the spiritual community," Mickey reached out and pulled Jolie into the RV. "You'll have to excuse us, Tru, but we've got a fitting to do." Jolie felt a spike of vengeful enjoyment as she was whisked past the disapproving Mae.

Her sense of victory was short-lived.

"I can't wear this." Jolie looked down at the long white gown as Iris pinched and tucked, pinning things into place. "It's like I'm Princess Leia trying to do Dragonball Z." She flapped her arms, her hands swallowed by a half yard of material. "The arms are too long, the waist is too short, the neck sags, and I'm going to break my leg on this skirt."

"You're quite a bit smaller than last year's maiden," Iris muttered around the pins in her mouth. "I'll just pin it up here...and here, and fold this over. I can take a tuck in the shoulders. Can't have our virgin's dress falling off in the middle of the ceremony."

"Don't worry, Jolie." Mickey fluffed a crown of greens. "Iris used to be a clothes designer back in New York. She can do anything with fabric."

Jolie eyed the crown skeptically.

"Couldn't I just wear a white tee shirt and jeans and dump the sheet? You can put a big 'V' on my forehead so everyone will know who I'm supposed to be."

"It's not a Halloween party, Ms. Figg," Mae snarled as she entered. "Maybe you should just concentrate on not causing any more trouble, eh?"

"Out," Iris barked sharply. "Go take care of something else, Mae. This is handled."

"Everything's fine, Mae, really," Mickey added, trying to sooth over Iris' harshness. Mae snorted and slammed the door behind her. Mickey began bundling the sleeves up to uncover Jolie's hands. "Don't mind Mae. She always gets this way around ceremony."

"You mean bitchy?"

"We use the term 'forceful,' but yeah." Iris continued making alterations.

"So how is Faith doing? Have you heard anything?" Jolie asked, cautiously.

Mickey hesitated. "She's still in the hospital. They were going to release her but she said she still felt woozy so they kept her another night."

But you don't believe her. Jolie sensed something Mickey wasn't saying. *Why?*

Mickey's head whipped around and she looked hard at Jolie. Jolie pretended not to notice.

"What Faith told me, was that she wasn't ready to go home yet," Iris corrected.

Which meant she'd miss the ceremony, leaving it all to Mae and Rory; the King and Queen of Misrule.

Jolie glanced at Mickey to see if she had picked Iris' thought up, but Mickey was still watching Jolie closely; too closely.

"So, what do you think happened, Jolie?" She asked with feigned casualness. "You were there, right?" *No one else saw anything except you,* Mickey added, silently.

Chapter Fifteen

Jolie went very still inside. Had Mickey just thought that to herself like people do, or was she testing her?

"What were you doing banging on her window in the middle if the night anyway?" Iris mumbled around pins. "You could kill an old lady, scaring her like that."

I wasn't the one trying to kill her, Jolie thought. "I was just trying to wake her up," she explained. "What someone ought to be asking, is what were Sean and Rick doing out there in the shed in the middle of the night?"

Iris stopped, the pins hanging out of her red-lipsticked mouth. "Sean and Rick were there?"

"Yeah. Out in back doing something weird, I don't know, a spell or something. I guess Mae skipped over that part, huh?" Jolie said bitterly.

Mickey placed a hand on Iris' arm as if to silence her. "What exactly did you see, Jo?" she asked gently.

Jolie considered how she should answer. Trusting these women was risky. If they truly were Rory's allies she would be revealing herself to him--something Faith had told her not to do. On the other hand, they seemed to genuinely care about Faith, and Jolie could use an ally or two about now. "When I first got there, Sean was in the shed chanting something inside a circle with a black candle in the middle. Then Rick showed up." Jolie looked straight at Mickey. *And that was when the black fog began coming toward the house.* Mickey looked alarmed. Jolie went on, "Things started feeling really creepy and I freaked. I didn't know what else to do, so I woke Faith up the only way I could."

Mickey's eyes were dark, round circles in her pale face, but she still remained silent.

"You were right to go to Faith," Iris agreed. "She's a good woman. She understands these things."

"How about you, Iris? Do you understand these things?" Jolie challenged her. "Or you Mickey? Because

I'm pretty confused right now. If you have any understanding or gifts, I don't see how you could let someone put Faith in danger and not do anything about it? And what about all of these people?" Jolie waved her hand to indicate the Solstice celebrants outside. "Don't you feel any responsibility toward them? Mickey, your little girls are here tonight for God's sake. Do you really think they're safe with Rory in charge?"

Mickey looked like she was choking on invisible words. Her mouth moved but nothing came out.

"Leave Mickey alone, Jolie," Iris growled. "Stop badgering her."

"Or what, Iris? You'll stick me with a pin? Please." Jolie turned her attention back to Mickey. "You're psychic, right, Mickey? You hear things? You heard my thoughts a few minutes ago, I know you did."

Mickey stepped over, closed the RV door, and leaned against it, panting as if she'd just run a marathon.

"Are you okay, Mick?" Iris stood ready to come to her friend's aid.

Mickey held up her hand to stop her. "I'm fine. Everything's fine."

Iris turned to Jolie, examining her with steely eyes.

"So that's it? You're gifted. That's why Faith took such an interest in you that first day?"

"Yeah, so? It doesn't make me a saint or raise my SAT scores. Mostly it just gets me into trouble."

"You have to learn to manage it."

"You mean like you do? Or like Mickey here? If you've been hearing people's thoughts, you had to have guessed something was wrong. I felt it the first moment I saw the guy. Rory is bad news. Why didn't you say anything?"

"Nothing is wrong. Everything is fine," Mickey repeated woodenly.

Chapter Fifteen

"The hell it is! Rory's been working to get Faith out of the way, and now he's got what he wanted, and no one knows what comes next. Unless you're keeping silent about that, too?"

"Don't be ridiculous. Sean loves his grandmother. He would never do anything to hurt her," Iris said.

"I wasn't talking about Sean. I was talking about Rory."

Now Iris' mouth began to move with no sound coming out.

"What are you trying to say, Iris?" Jolie watched her struggle. "Something about Rory?" She turned to Mickey. "Mickey?"

Mickey shook her head. "Sean would never..."

"I got that part; Sean would never do anything to hurt his grandmother. What about Rory?" Neither woman spoke, but their faces were set in determined grimaces. There was a battle going on inside them. "You can't say anything bad about him, can you?" The answer dawned on Jolie." You physically can't get the words out, even if you think them."

This was magic; real magic, not the mumbo jumbo wand flicking that Hollywood made up, but actual mental coercion. Was that even possible in a modern world? Part of Jolie was sure, like Father Owen, that there had to be some logical explanation, but the other part of her had seen the black fog rolling towards Mae's house.

Iris began shaking like she'd just been fished out of a frozen lake.

When a spell is threatened and its being weakened, those under its power can often be recognized by their uncontrollable trembling, Jolie heard Mickey thinking something she had heard or read. Mickey spun like a puppet unwinding on twisted strings, her face contorted. "How do we know that you're not the liar, Jolie Figg?"

Jolie pulled Faith's silver goddess out from under her shirt and held it out.

"That's Faith's," Iris muttered.

"She gave it to me that first day to protect me..." Jolie paused. "...From Rory. He's not who he says he is. But then you know that, don't you?"

"I thought I was the only one." Mickey gasped for breath. "Everyone else thought he was so wonderful. I told myself it was my ego and I should just be grateful for the chance to learn from him."

"I...could...never...say...anything," Iris choked out the words one at a time. "I tried a few times but everything just came out...scrambled."

"He's been manipulating you, and now that he's got Faith out of the way, he's ready to make his next move. Any ideas what that will be?"

"Showing your true colors, Ms. Figg?" The RV door had opens and Mae was standing in the doorway, accompanied by a chill blast of winter air. "Saying hateful things about a man who has never done you any harm is small minded and cruel. You've brought dissension and doubt among us on this blessed night. I'll inform Rick that he can take you home."

"Cool." Jolie wriggled out of the white dress and let it drop to the floor.

"But I was almost finished with the dress," Iris protested.

Mickey found her voice. "Who'll be our virgin, Mae?"

Mae sniffed. "The maiden symbolizes purity. I don't believe Ms. Figg fits that description." She exited in a swish of silk.

Chapter Fifteen

"Guess I'm out of here. Think about what I said. It's your circus now, ladies." Jolie headed for the door. Her feet hit the dirt and she sprinted back toward the parking lot where she'd last seen Rick.

"Jolie! Hey, Jolie!" a familiar voice stopped her. "I knew you'd be here." Rebecca panted, catching up.

"What are you doing here?" Jolie pulled her friend to the edge of the crowd.

"I came with some friends from the coffee shop. Look, Jo, I'm really sorry about all that stuff at school. I shouldn't have trusted those girls. I don't know what came over me. It was like I was under a spell or something."

Jolie cracked. "Oh my God! Do you hear yourself? You're such a friggin idiot, Rebecca. This isn't one of your fantasy books. No one made you do anything. You caved to peer pressure; that's all. You saw something shiny, and you dropped what you had in order to pick it up. It wasn't courageous or brave and there sure as hell wasn't anything magical about it."

Baby fat muffined over the top of Rebecca's jeans. Her thighs looked like they were trying to burst through the denim like seed pods. Her hair was unfashionably curly and her faded hoodie read: "I'm silently correcting your grammar." Her ten-minute brush with the "in crowd" had been a lapse in judgment, that was all, but she was never going to sit at the in table in the Barbie Dream House. In a few years, though, after she graduated and went away to college, she would discover that all the stuff kids thought were important in high school wasn't; the geeks were going to inherit the earth, and she was going to be okay.

Jolie bit her lip. "Look, I'm getting out of here now, and if you have any sense, you'll do the same. This is not a good place to be tonight."

"Really? Well, being such an idiot, I think I'll stay." Rebecca jerked her chin up and stomped off through the crowd.

It had not been Jolie's best moment. "You're so good with people," she muttered under her breath as she continued walking to the parking lot.

Rick wasn't where she'd seen him last, or anywhere in sight. She scanned the parked cars for signs of a flickering Bic or the smell of pot, then realized her soda had kicked in, and she hadn't peed since before she'd left the trailer. She looked back toward the ceremonial grounds. The only port-a-potty was by the entrance. Reluctant as she was to expose her tender places to the creepy crawlies of the desert, it was a better option than running into Rory. She walked past the parked cars and out into the desert. Ducking behind a boulder, she pulled her jeans and unders down as one unit and squatted. She was headed back when a voice came out of the darkness.

"We should talk." Sean was sitting on a nearby boulder, whittling a bit of wood with his pocket knife. Jolie looked back to where she had just been squatting with her jeans around her ankles.

"Did you follow me out here?"

"I didn't watch." He closed the knife and put it and the wood in his pocket. "Look, I'm worried about you. Stuff's going on."

"No shit. How long did it take you to figure that one out, Sherlock?"

"Hey, when did I become the enemy? Wasn't I the guy taking punches for you last night?"

"You kind of look like him, but you also look a lot like the jerk that was helping my mom's pedophile ex-boyfriend chase me down a few hours later."

"How could you think--? Man, you are one messed up chick, Jolie Figg."

Chapter Fifteen

Jolie held up a finger. "No, one smart chick. Smart enough to ask questions when stuff looks hinky, and stuff looked pretty damn hinky last night. What were you and Rick doing together in Mae's shed anyway?"

"We weren't together."

"You were there; he was there. What would you call it?"

"He showed up. I didn't invite him."

"And the lines you drew on the floor were for ring-around-the-rosy. Give me a break."

"I'm not on trial here, Jo, but since you asked so nice, Faith asked me to do something for her."

"What kind of something?"

"I don't know, some kind of protection thing. I'm not into this stuff, I just follow directions."

"A protection spell with a black candle?"

"You watch too many bad movies," Sean grumbled. "I would never do anything to hurt my grandmother."

"So I've been told. If you're not into magic and you would never hurt your grandmother, why are you hanging around Rick, and why were you chasing me last night?"

"I told you, I wasn't."

"It sure looked like it."

"It looked like you scared my grandmother and gave her a heart attack, too, but I knew that wasn't true. Why? Because I have faith in you." And she hadn't, Jolie got it. "I only came tonight because Faith asked me to look after her interests," Sean explained.

"What does that mean?" Jolie demanded, turning around and peering into the darkness to try to see his face. He just looked at her. "You mean me? Faith sent you to look after me?" She was going to have to think about that awhile. "You know, if you're lying to me, I'm going to punch you, right?" she muttered.

"I'm not lying. I wouldn't do that to you."

Jolie leaned back against the boulder, looking up at the starlit sky. A deep breath cleared her head and her lungs. Things were not what she'd feared; Sean was still Sean and not some jerkwad Rick Jr. The stars seemed a little brighter.

"I'm sorry if I..." she started.

"You didn't," he cut her off. "You're annoyingly prickly and uppity as hell, but you're also loyal, and honest, and the strongest person I know, outside of Faith," his lips stopped making words but his mind went on. *But then she doesn't have your crazy colored eyes, or that wild hair, or those lips that just beg to be kissed.*

Jolie's knees felt like jelly. If she closed her eyes, she and Sean could just have been two young people sitting on a porch, talking about nothing and toying with the idea of falling in love, but she didn't live in a world that was that simple.

"It wasn't cool, me leaving you at the house like that," she said. "I'm sorry. I just couldn't stay there anymore."

"I know," Sean said, his voice like thick warmed honey. "I was scared too."

"I wasn't scared," she protested.

"Shhh." Sean put a finger to her lips. He was so close she could smell the dust and sage scents clinging to him from his bike ride through the desert. "Apology accepted." He pulled her into his arms, raised her face to his and kissed her.

She hadn't expected it--not after all the times they'd felt the pull of attraction but stepped back from the precipice. Now it curled around them, pressing their bodies together and twining their breath. Jolie felt the pulse of his heart through her palms as they rested

Chapter Fifteen

against his chest. His lips were soft and strong and she wanted to stay here forever.

This is what safe feels like, she thought. For a moment, she had the sense that she and Sean had been here before, many times, then, just as suddenly as he'd pulled her into him, he let her go. She stumbled and caught herself on the edge of the boulder, as stunned by his absence as she'd been by his sudden closeness.

"Anyone can make a mistake once," he said hoarsely. "So, you were at Mae's last night because you were running away, is that it? You trusted Faith. That's good, Jo--smart. She'd never let you down."

Jolie shook her head to clear it. What was he doing talking about his grandmother? They needed to talk about what had just happened, didn't they? Jolie looked up at him. If he kissed her again, she would be his, body and soul forever, and he knew it too. The pain of it was scratched across his eyes.

God, you're such an idiot, Sean! He berated himself. *"What were you thinking? You should never have done that. She's just a kid; a frightened vulnerable kid who thinks you can solve all her problems--and you can't even solve your own. You can't ever let that happen again.* Jolie could see him steel himself. She felt like she was stumbling forward into a dark pit.

It was a kiss one kiss. Not a confession of undying love, a voice inside her head scolded. *Buck up and stop acting like a schoolgirl with her first crush.* Grown up people kissed each other all the time, it didn't change their lives or turn the sky pink.

"Oh, I almost forgot. This is for you." Sean's hand shook as he took a piece of paper from his pocket. The number was written on hospital note paper. "It's Faith's cell number. She said you should use it whenever you needed to--if you had questions, or there was something you didn't understand, or you just needed to talk."

Jolie pulled herself together. "Great. We can exchange recipes." She put the note in her pocket. Had Faith known this was going to happen? Had she "seen" it?

"You okay?" Sean asked.

"Sure." Jolie tried to gather up some of her prickly bits and piece them back together. "But you probably shouldn't make a habit of kissing everyone who apologizes to you. It could get awkward."

"Right." Sean grinned. "Well, I uh, need to go. I promised Faith a full report. You'll be all right here?"

"Absolutely." *When have I not?* she thought bitterly.

"Keep away from Rick and Rory, okay?" Sean started back toward the ceremonial grounds.

"Don't worry about me," Jolie quipped, looking around at the barren desert. Outside of the fire at the ceremonial grounds, there wasn't a light for miles. "I'll be fine out here in the dark, in the desert, all alone. What could possibly go wrong?"

CHAPTER SIXTEEN

Jolie picked her way around the outer edge of the low circle of hills that surrounded the ceremonial grounds, coming up the back side, farthest away from the parking lot where people were still socializing. No way was she going to get caught sitting around in the dark hugging her knees while everything went sideways. If stuff was going to come down, she wanted to see it coming so she would know whether to dodge and run or stand and fight.

When she was little, Mem sometimes had Jolie help her fill the little mojo bags people came to her for and she always made a point of focusing only on good things while they worked. If something negative came up, she burned that bag.

"There's other stuff in here that's important," Mem explained. "But your intent is the most important thing. It's like a little bit of you--like your wish, or what you're asking the universe to give this person. You can't see intent, but you can always feel it. That's the reason people come to our family for their protections. They know the Boulet's intent is only for the good."

Mem had always been very serious about the family's reputation. She wouldn't do a bag or a blessing for just anybody. If she didn't know you and you came asking for something, she had to meet you first, and decide if you were okay or not. If she didn't get a good feeling about you, you were politely shown the door.

"You're not going to help him, Mem?" Jolie had asked the first time she saw her grandmother refuse someone.

"Some people you just can't help, Jolie." Mem shook her head. "And it's just going to hurt you both if you try."

Jolie thought about this as she climbed up the low hill in the desert and lay down on her belly, craning her neck to peek over into the ceremonial grounds. If intent was so important, what was Rory's intent tonight?

Whatever he wanted to do, it was not part of the usual ceremony to call back the Light, and it couldn't be done with just the coven ladies and a few of their friends. It needed lots of people to work, and Faith would never have allowed it.

Though Jolie didn't think Rory was half as gifted as he pretended to be, he did know something, the coven ladies' enchantment was proof of that, and whatever he knew, was more than someone without a conscience had a right to.

Jolie watched as the last of the participants began to move into the ceremony area. Rory and Mae were just below her, opposite the entrance into the ceremonial area. Jolie couldn't hear what they were saying, but the discussion was clearly working into an argument. Mae kept pointing at Rick, then off towards the parking lot. Finally, Rory said something to Rick and Rick marched away through the crowd. Jolie hoped he wasn't looking for her.

Jolie scooted back from the top of the hill and checked the barren landscape to see how exposed she was. Marty was climbing toward her.

"So what are we doing here?" the big guy asked, cheerfully.

"Get down! Get down!" Jolie motioned to him.

"What? Why?" He dropped to his belly onto the stony ground. "Why are we hiding?"

"I don't want them to see us."

Chapter Sixteen

"Right." He scanned the area below. "Tru sent me to find you. So tell me again why you're out here and everyone else is down there? 'Cause I thought you were the sacrificial virgin or something."

"My understudy's replacing me."

"Oh. Aren't allowed to play with the other kiddies, eh? What did you do, pull the black cat's tail?"

"I don't think I like the game."

"Well, it's not Christmas, there's no Santa Clause or anything, but in my experience, these things are usually pretty harmless."

"I'm not so sure this time."

"Why? What's going on, Kid?"

Jolie didn't answer.

"You know, Tru's down there, right? Now, I'm a pretty easy going guy most of the time, but if something happens to her and you could have stopped it, I'm gonna be pissed."

"Yeah, I got that."

"So tell me, what's got you so worried so I can decide what I'm going to do about it."

Jolie studied Marty. "Okay. Do you see that guy over there?" She pointed out Rory. "He's taking over the ceremony tonight."

"The sleazy game show host dude?"

"Yeah, that's him."

"Where's the old lady?"

"Faith is in the hospital under suspicious circumstances."

"What do you mean suspicious?"

"The explanation you'll get from her daughter in law, Mae," Jolie pointed her out. "Is that some teenage delinquent, namely me, banged on Faith's window last night and gave her a heart attack."

"Last night? Is that where we took you? Not cool, Jolie. We didn't know..."

"Wait. The real answer is that there was some really weird stuff going on--stuff that I think had to do with Rory wanting to run this thing tonight. I got worried that Faith was in danger and had to warn her really fast. The window was just an innocent bystander."

Marty rubbed the back of his neck. "I'm going to go get Tru." Marty scrambled back down the slope and headed towards the RV.

He was already too late. While they'd been talking, the participants had been called to gather. Tru was on the East side of the circle, her maroon hair marking her like a beacon.

"Marty!" Jolie hissed, but he was too far away to hear her. "Marty!" She raised her voice as Rick came around the opposite side of the hill.

"There you are. I've been given special instructions for you, little miss." He smiled creepily.

"Give me the keys and I'll go to the truck and wait for you," Jolie said, getting up and dusting herself off. "That way you can go back to the ceremony and not have to miss anything."

"I ain't givin' you my keys. What do you think I am, stupid?"

Jolie didn't answer.

"I've got a better idea. I'm going to tie you up so you can't cause me any more trouble. Then I'll know exactly where to find you when I'm done here, and I can give you my full attention." He grabbed her arm and began marching her to the parking lot.

Jolie wanted to scratch his eyes out, but she held herself in check. She needed Rick to believe she wasn't going to cause problems.

Chapter Sixteen

"Come on, Rick, give me a break," she whined. "You don't need to tie me up. Where am I gonna go? We're in the middle of nowhere. Why would I want to run off? Everything between here and civilization is sharp and thorny, or it bites. I'm a city girl. I'd be lost in two seconds."

"Yeah. Don't forget that."

"You just go do your thing, and when you're done, I'll be waiting for you here in the truck. Mom will probably be home by the time we get back," she added, hoping he didn't remember what she'd said earlier about her mom wanting to break up. It wasn't much to a creep like Rick, but the thin connection between he and Jessie was the only protection Jolie had at the moment.

He stopped by his El Camino and looked Jolie up and down slowly.

"You're trying pretty hard to convince me. Just how hard are you willing to try?"

It was a question she could not possibly answer right, no matter what she said.

"Not that hard," she opted for honesty, holding her hands out to him to be tied.

Rick pulled some rope out of the back of his truck, tied her hands together, then pushed her inside.

"If I have to come back here to tell you to be quiet, I'm gonna be pissed, and if you manage to find a way to not be here when I'm ready to leave, I'm leaving you out here and you can walk home. You understand?"

"Screw you, asshole," Jolie muttered.

Rick slapped her across the face and pushed her so that she fell backward onto the truck seat. He loomed over her, his long greasy hair half hiding his mad eyes. Jolie could feel the pent up waves of anger, frustration, and impotence flowing off of him. His fists were clenched and a nervous twitch pumped in his cheek.

Jolie held her breath, her heart racing. She'd gone too far. She shouldn't have shot off her mouth.

She'd read in a pamphlet from the Rape Crisis Center that rape wasn't about sex, it was about power. Rick would not violate her because he desired her, he would do it because he would be showing her he was more powerful than she was, and he wanted to hurt and humiliate her. The tension between them was terror drawn into a taut line. Her mouth was dry, but her eyes watered, and she hated that because he would think he'd made her cry.

If he takes one step closer, slam your foot into his balls and scream like bloody murder, she coached herself.

New Agey music began to blast from the tiny CD player at the ceremonial grounds. Things were starting.

"Hey, Rick, you coming?" one of his friends called from the edge of the parking lot.

"Yeah. I'll be right there," Rick shouted back. He pulled a dirty bandanna out of his pocket and tied it around Jolie's mouth. "You'll wait," he informed her, superiority coursing through his veins like a drug.

Jolie wanted to spit back, *No, I won't,* but her mouth was full of cotton.

Rick slammed the truck door, locked it and jogged off.

Jolie lay on the seat, trembling. A starry sky winked at her from just beyond the steering wheel.

I just need a minute, she thought as a tear slid from the corner of her eye, falling into the copper and pink strands of her hair. How many girls had lost their childhood with this view--a steering wheel and stars? How many babies had been made from lust, selfishness, or low self-esteem, instead of from love? Jolie's face

Chapter Sixteen

ached where Rick had hit her and she could not stop shaking.

Just put the pieces back together, she told herself. *It will be all right...any minute now; it will be all right.* Someday, there wouldn't be enough pieces left to put her back together in any functional way; like Humpty Dumpty in the kids' nursery rhyme. So many bits would be missing that the wind would just blow right through all the cracks and holes until she came apart, and that was that. Jolie set her jaw and sniffled. Someday; but not tonight.

She sat up, slipped her hands under the lock, pulled it up, and opened the door.

When she had offered her hands to Rick to be tied, he had been so deep into his own image of dominance over her, that he hadn't even thought about how stupid it was to tie her hands in front of her. Jolie pulled the bandana out of her mouth, wiped her face on her shirtsleeve, and walked across the parking lot towards the ceremonial grounds. Marty and Tru were walking toward her.

"What is this all about, Jolie?" Tru demanded. "Marty pulled me out of the circle, saying you'd explain."

Marty frowned at Jolie's hands. "What's with your hands, kid?"

"My mother's ex. I don't think he's taking the break up well."

"Here, let me." Marty untied her hands.

"Does one of you want to explain to me what's going on?" Tru asked.

Jolie looked at Marty.

"It's your gig, Jo."

"I'll try," Jolie explained what she knew as they walked back to her overlook on the hill.

Tru turned to Marty. "You realize this is completely insane, right? I'm sorry, Jo. I really like you, but..."

"You think she's lying," Marty finished.

Tru glanced at Jolie. "Well, not exactly, but how can she be telling the truth? I mean it's pretty out there."

"Look, I'm not asking you to believe me. I'm not asking for anything. Believe what you want. Do what you want, but FYI, I don't think you want to go back into that circle." Jolie flopped down on her belly and wriggled herself up to the top of the hill.

The participants were in place. Rory had put Mickey on his right--which made sense. In spite of her childlike innocence, or maybe because of it, she seemed to have the greatest gifts in the coven. Mae was on Rory's left. Claire and Iris were on either side of Mickey and Mae. Whatever Iris and Mickey had said to each other after Jolie left, they stood united now, their hands tightly clasped together.

Most of the people seemed to know what they were expected to do--or at least what they thought they were going to do. Jolie figured that Rory would begin things in the familiar way until people got comfortable, and then when they were into it, things would begin to change. She could see now, that some people were looking around, confused that Rory and Mae had taken the lead places. Faith McBride was nowhere to be seen. Those who had not heard about Faith's sudden illness got brief, whispered explanations. People listened and nodded, some looked reassured, others seemed nervous, but were unwilling to bring attention to themselves by walking out. It was too late for that. No one wanted to be the one to break the circle. They might not know this new person, but they trusted Faith McBride.

Jolie wished she'd thought to ask someone how the ceremony normally went, so she'd know what to look

Chapter Sixteen

for when Rory began to change it, but it was too late for that too.

The music from the CD player changed, and with it, the feeling of expectation from the crowd rose. Mae stepped forward and raised her hands, her long draping sleeves making her look like an ancient temple priestess- -which Jolie was sure was what she'd been going for. For some of the New Agers, this was like a second Halloween.

"As elder of the McBride clan," Mae began.

It should have been Faith.

She said she was feeling weak and wasn't ready to leave yet, Mickey had said. The doctor had told Faith that she could go home but Faith had refused, making it impossible for her be at the ceremony tonight or at home alone. What was she so worried about? If Faith thought something bad might happen here, why had she stepped back? She didn't seem like the cowardly type. People like Mem and Faith took their commitments very seriously, like some extraordinary sense of responsibility to humanity had been tattooed onto their souls before birth.

Jolie rubbed Faith's silver pendant between her fingers. How far would things have gone if Jolie had not come to the house and woken Faith up? Did Mae know Rory had attacked her mother-in-law? Was she under Rory's spell, an innocent bystander, or had she played a more sinister role in the plan? Would the fog have harmed only Faith, or would it have affected anyone it touched? If it couldn't be made specific, then Mae would have been in danger from it as much as Faith was. Would that have suited Rory's purposes just as well?

Mae was making her way around the circle, stopping occasionally to speak with a participant. Claire followed, swinging a brass incense burner. The scented smoke rose and drifted away on the air currents.

"Frankincense and myrrh," Tru whispered as she crawled up alongside Jolie. "It's been used since ancient times to purify before ceremonies."

"Hm. Like salt?"

"The rich man's version. We thought we'd come keep you company if that's okay? It's too late to join the circle now," Tru offered by way of an excuse. "And it's a good spot to see everything from."

"So you believe me?"

"Hold on, Nancy Drew, I didn't say that. I still hope you're wrong, but if you are right, you may need some backup."

"That's right, baby. Everybody needs back up," Marty repeated, cheerfully.

"Shut up, goofball," Tru punched his arm.

"Yes, dear." Marty winked at Jolie.

"Friggin Boy Scout."

With the cleansing of the circle complete, Mae and Claire returned to their places, and Mickey began to sing something wistful in a high sweet voice. Sean had placed himself outside the circle beside the CD player, apparently with the excuse that he would run it.

Jolie's attention went back to Rory. His lips were moving as if he were muttering something to himself. He looked around furtively to check if his actions were being watched.

From the corners of her eyes, Jolie caught movement out in the desert--shadows were slithering and sliding across the humped and broken hills, all of them headed toward the circle.

"What is that?" she turned and looked out across the desert.

Chapter Sixteen

"What's what?" Marty asked as he and Tru turned around as well.

"Did you see it?" Jolie asked, her heart pounding savagely.

"I didn't see anything. There's nothing out there but desert, Jo." Tru hesitated. "But I do feel something weird--like something's sort of wrong."

"Like in the horror films when you know they should start running," Jolie mused.

Marty chuckled. "But they never do."

Jolie squinted at the low hills, the open spaces, the shadows stalking the bushes, and the bizarre shapes made by the Joshua trees. All appeared silent and still. She looked back at Rory, focusing on what he was doing, and there it was again, lurking at the corners of her sight; a shadowy black fog. Twisted shapes tore at its edges, forming into clawed hands, feet, tails, and misshapen heads. Their yellow eyes glowed with hunger.

"Oh shit," Jolie muttered.

CHAPTER SEVENTEEN

"**W**e are so screwed," Jolie announced to Tru and Marty.

"Why? What's happening?" Tru asked. "I don't see anything."

"You can only see it out of the corner of your eye. Focus on something else--look at Rory."

Tru did. "I still don't see anything, even when I don't look at it." She peered into the darkness. "You really see something, Jolie? What is it?"

"I don't know." Jolie pulled out the piece of paper with Faith's number on it and punched it into her cell's keypad. The phone on the other end barely rang before someone answered.

"Hello?" Faith's voice was as thin as non-fat milk.

"Faith? It's Jolie."

"Thank God. I've been waiting for you to call," All pretense of weakness in Faith vanished. "Have they started?"

"Yeah. Faith, listen to me. The other night when I knocked on your window, I saw a black fog coming toward the house. I think Rory called it, and I think he's called it again. It's coming out of the desert. It's made up of creatures and things and it's headed for the ceremony.

"You see these creatures?" Faith asked.

"Sort of. If I look just right."

"Tell her that we can feel them," Tru interrupted.

"Who's that?" Faith demanded. "Is there someone there with you?"

"Yeah, Tru and Marty. They came to the ceremony."

Chapter Seventeen

"Why aren't they with the others?"

"I met them the other night on my way to your house. When I saw them here, I warned them things might get weird, so they came out here with me."

"That's good. You're not alone. Let me talk to one of them."

Jolie handed the phone to Tru. She could hear Faith talking, but she couldn't make out the words. Tru mostly just nodded, giving an occasional, "Yes, Ma'am." Like Sean said, people didn't argue with his grandmother. When Faith was done, Tru handed the phone back to Jolie.

"Can you put me on speaker on your phone?" Faith asked.

"Sure." Jolie did.

"Now listen to me, Jolie. I want you to close your eyes so you can see what's going on."

"That makes no sense, Faith..."

"Stop, Jolie, and listen to me. We don't have time for a proper lesson, so I need you to just do what I tell you. I'm going to give you a crash course in using your gifts to *see*. Do you understand?"

"Yes, Ma'am," Jolie answered.

Tru smiled, slid closer to Marty and took his hand.

"What's she talking about 'gifts'?" Marty whispered.

Tru shushed him. "It's Jolie. She's a psychic. That's why she can see things we can't."

"Cool," Marty grinned. "Maybe we should come to these things more often." Tru punched his arm.

"Let's just get through this one first, okay?"

"Close your eyes, Jolie, and focus your attention on the spot on your forehead between your eyebrows," Faith instructed. "*Seeing* energy has little to do with using your physical eyes. Most of the time they just get in the way; that's why you can see the creatures from the corners of your eyes, but not when you look directly at them."

"How did you know--?" Jolie started to ask.

"Explanations can come later--I hope."

The small confirmation was reassuring; the "I hope" less so.

"Our physical vision is linked by habit to the logical part of our brains," Faith went on. "So it's always trying to take what we see and fit it into a familiar framework. Only with the spiritual world, it mostly just gets it wrong, so you need to resist trying to make sense of what you *see* and just accept it; like in a dream. Now focus your attention on the spot between your brows. Think about relaxing and expanding there. This spot is called the third eye, and it is used for *seeing*. Notice that as you relax it, the circle there opens wider and wider. Use your breath and think about widening it on every exhale."

"These four women represent the four stages of life," Mae's voice addressed the crowd, cutting through the airy music.

Jolie's eyes flew open.

Mae was gesturing for the four women to step into the center of the circle. The youngest was a child, one of Mickey's daughters. Mickey followed her closely, protective and proud, then Claire stepped in. She was followed by Rebecca wearing the Princess Leia dress.

"Crap," Jolie fumed under her breath. In spite of the fact that she had not done anything to encourage Rebecca to come, she felt responsible for her being here.

"What?" Marty asked.

"My understudy down there is a girl I know from high school."

Chapter Seventeen

"If you're right about all this, it's going to suck to be you on Monday."

"You're telling me," Jolie agreed.

Mae directed the four females to make a circle facing outward.

"Tru, does everything look normal with the ceremony?" Faith asked over the phone.

"Yes."

Marty squeezed Tru's hand. "I don't see anything strange, but then all I've got is regular old eyes," he said.

"That's good," Faith assured him. "Someone needs to keep watch in the physical world as well. A *seer* is very vulnerable when they're focused on other worlds. Do it now, Jolie."

Jolie closed her eyes and tried to focus on *seeing*, using only her inner sight.

"The child, the maiden, the mother, and the crone," Rory's voice took over. "We honor each stage of life for each has its time, place, and lessons for our lives. Take a moment to reflect on where you are at this turning of the year, the path you have traveled since the last Solstice and those who walked with you. Consider your own loved ones. Perhaps they are challenged by the changes they face, their health, or a loss. At this powerful time year, we have much to give."

Mae instructed the women in the center to stretch out their arms toward the crowd.

"Send the love and healing you would send your loved ones to these four women," Rory commanded the crowd. "Focus on channeling your energy to them."

"Okay, that last part was new," Tru announced. "He's changing it."

Most of the people in the circle had their eyes closed now. They reached their arms out to the Circle of Four in the center, imagining sending them the energy they wished to send their absent loved ones. Some of them could even do it--not Rebecca of course, but no one else would notice. Jolie began to see thin streams of light shooting to and from the four in the center.

"Move your circle clockwise," Rory ordered the coven women in the outer circle. They tugged their neighbors into motion until the whole circle moved as one. The new-agers were eating it up. Love and light; they had replaced "good luck" and "see you later," but their belief in warm fuzzies had no place in the world Jolie woke up in every day.

Mae nodded to Sean and he punched a button on the CD player, changing the music to a chant with a steady, dominant drumbeat. Movement, music, and chanting; the classic elements of trance worship, were now in place. Rory had them. They were connecting. Rebecca shuffled along looking out of place.

Jolie could see lines of energy growing, as bright as neon, drawn across the screen of her closed eyelids, like the spokes of a wheel running from the crowd to the four females in the center, from three of them to the coven ladies, and from there to Rory. Rebecca's "spoke" was simply not there.

"He's taking the energy from the crowd into himself," Jolie explained. "But Why? What's he going to do with it all?"

Rory stiffened and a dead-blank closed over his face. His body convulsed and hose-shaped tubes, like large coarse hairs, erupted from the line following his spine. A dark creature scrambled over the hill. Leaping up behind Rory, it grabbed one of the tubes and began sucking from it.

"Oh, gross!"

"What? What's happening?" Marty demanded.

Chapter Seventeen

"You don't want to know." Jolie looked beyond the circle out into the desert with her sightless eyes. Creatures were flowing toward them, leaping, and crawling, each trying to outrun the others. They were mashed together in one huge black mass. The desert floor was alive with them, coming from every direction. They swarmed over the low rolling hills like the plagues of locusts in the old Bible movies she had seen, but Jolie didn't think these creatures had anything to do with God. She opened her eyes and turned again, looking out across an apparently empty desert. She closed them again, trying to wrap her mind around the scope of what she was seeing.

"There must be thousands," she whispered. She opened her eyes.

"Are you okay, Jo?" Marty and Tru moved closer.

"They're coming like a flood." She pulled away from her friends, sitting up, shaking out her arms and hands. This could not be real. It could not be happening. Everything felt mixed up, confused, upside-down, and inside out.

"Tru, what's going on?" Faith asked through the phone. "Is Jolie all right?"

Tru moved over to Jolie's and stopped her, taking Jolie's face between her hands.

"Are you?"

"It's real, what I'm seeing?" Jolie asked. "Nobody gave me something to make me hallucinate or something?"

"I'm sorry, I know it must be frightening," Faith said gently. But I need you to be brave and look at it, even though it's hard. I can only help if I know what you're seeing because no one else sees it but you."

Looking like she was facing a firing squad, Jolie rolled back over and closed her eyes.

There was a creature feeding from every tube coming out of Rory's back now, and more of the creatures were arriving every second, pushing, and clawing. Even with all the energy, he was taking from the others in the circle, there would not be enough for all of them to feed. Like a pack of starving carnivores, the creatures snorted, ripped, and tore at each other until stringy black body parts littered the ground.

Jolie curled up and gagged.

"Jolie! Open your eyes, Jolie," Marty ordered as she began to lose consciousness.

"What's happening?" Faith shouted through the phone.

"She's passing out."

"Tell her to open her eyes," Faith commanded.

"Open your eyes, Jolie. Come on. Come back," Tru rubbed the girl's hands and cheeks.

"Make her open her eyes," Faith was adamant. "Can you see the creatures, Tru?"

"No, Ma'am." She glanced up quickly, her own eyes bugging out. "Oh God, Ms. McBride, I think some of them are looking this way. I saw yellow eyes."

"Wake her up, now!"

"Jolie, open your eyes, Goddamit! Jolie," Marty shook Jolie until her eyelids fluttered open.

"They're open!" Tru shouted.

"Thank God," Faith breathed from the phone. "That should stop the creatures' interest, Tru."

"Okay." Tru eyed the desert which again looked empty and brown.

Jolie wiped her mouth, her eyes dark with terror. "I can't do this. I don't know anything about any of this stuff. I hear what people think sometimes, that's all. It doesn't make me powerful, or special, or important. It just makes me scared."

Chapter Seventeen

"Well, thank God for that. It shows you've got good sense. Give me that thing." Marty grabbed the phone from Jolie's hand. "This is too much for her," he told Faith. "Jolie's not you. She's just a kid. She can't do this by herself."

"She's not by herself. You're there, Tru and Marty, and yes, she can do this," Faith insisted. "She has to because there is no one else."

"You could..."

"Do you think if I could that I would be there? I don't have Jolie's gifts, and I don't have the physical strength left to fight something like this." Faith's voice cracked. "If something's going to be done, Jolie is the only one with any chance of doing it."

Jolie shook her head. "There are too many. You'd need an army of wizards, or psychics, or something to have any chance of fighting this, Faith."

Marty looked out at the empty desert. "I still don't see anything."

"You just keep watching out for me and Jolie, okay, Honey?"

"You can count on me." Marty kissed Tru. "I love you, Tru."

"I love you, too, Marty." Tears streaked Tru's cheeks. "Who'd have thought one little runaway could cause so much trouble, huh?"

"She didn't cause the trouble," Marty pointed out. "If it weren't for Jolie, we'd be down there with the rest of the sacrificial lambs."

"I'm sorry." Jolie looked as if she were about to cry. "I'm just one girl."

"Bullshit!" Faith swore. "You are Lucy Boulet's granddaughter, and that means you have a gift. Gifted people are not born into this world by accident, Jolie. There are reasons they come. They have responsibilities.

You may not know what they are yet because you are still young, but none of this is by chance. Stop thinking that all you have to do is open your eyes and all the bad things will go away. It's not true. It's all still there. The only difference is, you can't see it. But not seeing it doesn't mean it won't affect things. What you see in that other world crosses over, whether you see it or not. If you do not help these people tonight, Jolie, I can't say what will happen to them in this physical world, but in the morning they won't just be going home to their families, well and happy. There will be consequences." Her voice cracked. "And it's my fault they're there. They trusted me. Please don't let this tragedy be my legacy, Jo."

Jolie shook her head. "I'm not Obi Wan Kenobi or some sorcerer prodigy. I'm just me."

"That's good enough for me." Marty smiled.

Jolie looked from Tru to Marty to the ceremonial grounds then out to the empty desert that she knew was not empty. She took a deep breath.

"What the hell. I'm not going to be able to get a ride until this thing's all over with anyway." Marty gripped Jolie's shoulders and gave them a squeeze. She didn't mind.

"Tru, can you see Sean?" Faith asked.

"Yes."

"Is he connected to the circle?"

"No."

"Good boy. Tell that boyfriend of yours to go fetch him and bring him back."

"I'm not leaving Tru," Marty argued.

"We can't leave Jolie here alone, Marty. Just hurry, okay, honey? I'll be right here when you get back. I promise."

Chapter Seventeen

"Okay, Babe. But you stay put, okay?" Marty trotted off, taking the short cut over the hill. Chances were none of the dazed creatures in the circle would notice him since he was unconnected and very much alive.

"Feel better, Jo?" Faith's voice crackled from the phone, missing half the syllables. The battery was running down.

"I'm okay." Jolie's breathing was normal again and the nausea had lessened.

"Good. Close your eyes and tell me what you see."

Jolie closed her eyes and groaned. "It's gotten worse. Rory is drawing energy from the crowd through the four women in the center and the coven women, and the creatures are fighting over who feeds." Rebecca had joined in. Her energy was now connected. Jolie felt a surge of protective anger. "They better leave her alone," she growled.

"Turn," Rory commanded the four women in the center of the circle. "Counterclockwise."

The inner circle began to shuffle step sideways, rotating their circle within the circle in the opposite direction from the crowd. Jolie could hear the energy shrieking, like some giant rusty machine's gears being stripped.

"Something's changing, Faith," Tru said, alarmed.

"Big time," Jolie agreed. There was no reply. "Faith? Faith?" Both women looked at the phone. It had gone dead. "Shit!" Jolie threw it onto the ground. Raking her fingers through her hair, she tried to gather herself together and figure out what to do next. "We're on our own," she announced.

CHAPTER EIGHTEEN

The dark creatures continued to pour over the hills and onto the ceremonial grounds, climbing over their brethren like ants. Whatever Rory knew or did not know about the powers he had set in motion, instinct urged him to reach out for help. Blindly, he grabbed Rick, pulling him to his side.

"I need you here, with me," he said, his lips pale.

"Sure, Rory."

Seeker lines popped out of Rory's belly, looking for somewhere to attach. Sensing a threat, Rick pulled back.

"Don't move," Rory growled. With a strength greater than his own, he held Rick in place. The adder-like heads of the seeker lines tracked like dogs, sniffing the air, then leaped across the space between the two men, tunneling into Rick's mid-section. He had asked to be taught; now he would pay the price.

Instantly, feeder tubes sprouted along Rick's spine and popped out his back. The ravenous horde surged forward. Behind Rick, a familiar dark, monkey-like ink blot of a shadow jumped up and down hissing and squeaking at the usurpers feeding on its slave and master.

Fresh seeker lines wriggled out of the double blob of energy that was now the merged Rick-Rory, searching again. Rory's dark followers and those who were most unprotected were the creature's first targets. The coven ladies' connection, established and strengthened over months, was strong, and they suffered now as Rory and Rick took energy from them without reserve. Rory reached out to Mae as he had to Rick, and in moments

Chapter Eighteen

she looked like a potato sprouting in the sack with roots coming out of her back and dozens of creatures battling to the death to feed off her.

Marty grabbed Sean and raced back across the circle, ducking under arms and weaving through connected bodies to avoid contact, Rick reached out for Sean's arm.

"Sean, watch out!" Jolie shouted. Sean landed a hard right hook on Rick's jaw and Rick fell, his eyes rolling back into this head. Jolie turned away, not wanting to watch what the creatures would do to him.

Neither Iris nor Mickey seemed to see the black things but their energy connections to Rory were continuing to weaken, both visibly shaking.

My babies. I have to get to my babies, Jolie heard Mickey's silent scream.

Hurry, Mickey. Hurry. Fight him. Jolie shouted, silently. *Iris, break out. Mickey needs you.* Mickey's daughter and Becca were all but gone; their faces blank, eyes vacant, barely able to stand, and Jolie did not know how much longer they would be able to last before they lost consciousness. *Hold on. Just hold on,* she tried to encourage them.

"Jolie!" Sean called her.

Jolie opened her eyes to see Sean climbing the hill toward her. Focusing on his blue eyes, she rose and stumbled across the rocky ground and threw herself into his arms, sobbing. In spite of what he had told himself earlier about staying away from her, his arms folded protectively around her, making a small safe haven in the midst of all the darkness.

"Are you okay, Jo?" Sean asked. "Did something happen? Did someone hurt you?"

"Just hold me for a minute, okay? You don't have to do anything else, just stand there." She held onto his shirt and breathed him in, reliving that feeling of being safe. She wondered if, after tonight, she would ever feel that way again. Then, taking a deep breath, she set her fear aside, squared her shoulder, and stepped back.

"Okay, I'm ready." *I'm a Boulet. I can do this*, she told herself.

"For the next few hours, I need you to trust me, Sean and do what I say. Okay?"

"Okay," Sean said hesitantly.

"See?" Tru nudged Marty. "She is a Boulet."

"If you're saying Jolie can kick some spiritual ass, I'm with you."

"Something's going on," Tru warned.

Rory had moved toward the edge of the inner circle and picked up a wooden bowl set there during preparations for the ceremony. Reaching into it with one hand, he brought out a fistful of black sand. As he walked in an arc, he let the sand sift through his fingers making a dark line on the ground.

"What's he doing?" Jolie asked.

"Beats me." Sean shrugged, still completely unaware of the scope of what they were dealing with.

"I've never seen this before," Tru agreed.

Jolie grimaced. "What do you usually do at these things, play Ring Around The Rosy to Celtic music?"

Marty chuckled. "Yeah, pretty much."

Tru punched him. "Somebody's gonna get their ass kicked when we get home."

Marty grinned.

"Do you have a phone with a signal, Sean?" Marty asked.

Sean pulled it out. "Two bars. Not much."

"Call your grandmother," Tru ordered him.

"Now? It's past midnight."

"Yes, now."

"She's up, Sean. Call her," Jolie agreed, still watching the action below.

Rory had reached the place where he'd started. Taking a step to the left he kept walking, not closing the circle.

It's not a circle, Jolie realized. "It's a spiral." She knew the symbol. It had been drawn on a cave wall in Chaco Canyon by the Anasazi Indians where the Solstice sun would shine on it once a year at dawn, after the longest night of winter.

"Is she answering?" Jolie asked Sean.

"There's not enough signal."

"Text."

"Text what? No one has told me what is going on."

Jolie looked at the bonfire just beyond the circle. It had burned low; its energy waning. *The longest night...when darkness was at its peak.* Did the fire just need a fresh log or was there something more it was trying to tell her? She looked around. The light was dimmer, but the creatures looked more solid and sharply etched against the darkness. Jolie looked back at the sand symbol on the ground.

"It goes the wrong way. He's drawing it backwards." She turned to Tru. "It's not a spiral of renewal and life, it's a spiral of destruction: death." Her logical brain did not want to accept that some deluded guy playing connect the dots in black sand could make bad things happen, but even with her eyes open now, things were beginning to bleed through and if she closed them--the world was chaos. Rory's intent had become clear.

"Shit. Give me that thing," Tru grabbed the phone from Sean's hand and began texting furiously.

The dark creatures were beating their chests, posturing, and parading before each other like gorillas showing off their strength. They hissed at each other and bared their teeth at any of their kind who ventured too close to their feeding source, then they turned, and pushed their way back in, and slurped away again.

The creatures feeding off Rick hopped up and down on his belly, jumping back and forth over his prone body, laughing when they landed on him. Others piled onto him pretending to ride him while newcomers fought for a chance at the feeding tubes.

Rory's dark entourage had a much harder time following him and feeding while he walked, as he spilled his spiral of death onto the sandy ground.

Rory's followers were beginning to have "fuel empty" signs in their eyes. What would it mean in the physical world if they were drained by these creatures? Faith had said there would be consequences, but she had not said what they were. Would people just be very sick or would there be more permanent damage?

"They're getting weak," Tru said quietly.

Jolie scanned the grounds, seeking out the faces of those she knew: Iris, Marty, her girls, Becca.

"Don't let this tragedy be my legacy" Faith had begged. It wasn't right. It wasn't fair. These people hadn't done anything wrong. They had just wanted to celebrate the Return of the Light, as their ancestors had for thousands of years.

"Jo?" Sean studied her, worriedly.

"Tell Faith she needs to send someone to help--send them now!"

"She did, honey," Tru said, softly. "She sent you." She held the phone so Jolie could see it. The text said: "Tell her she has all the help she needs."

The silver talisman around her neck burned against her chest. *"You are not alone,"* Jolie heard a voice made

Chapter Eighteen

up of many voices. It felt like the voices of the people in the birth dream. *"You never were."*

"You are a world away," Jolie answered.

"Not all of us." Far up on a ridge overlooking the circle, Jolie could see a distant speck of light. Another fire was burning in the desert. As Jolie focused on it; she suddenly found herself beside it, but it was not the fire that glowed. An old man with long salt and pepper braids looked up at her as if he could see her wandering spirit. He examined her with deep, seeing eyes, a vibrant glow radiating from him.

"We are all here," the voices whispered. *"You just can't see us with your eyes open."* Glints of energy were scattered across the desert and beyond.

Reluctantly, Jolie closed her eyes.

The never ending tide of darkness came on like the stormy crests of a turbulent black sea...Rory making his death spiral... Rick, a ball of human flesh served up as a banquet for demons.

"I see only evil," she said, sadly.

"Look again, Jolie," Tru urged her. "Look at Mickey and her girls. Look at their sweet little faces."

Jolie did. Mickey stood by her older child, wrapping the girl in nurturing green and pink heart-energy while sending another ribbon to cocoon the daughter that was opposite them in the circle. The strength of her innocence and unselfish motherly love made her strong, and in spite of the fading firelight, her spirit shone. There was Rebecca, too, fighting to stand, even though she had no idea what was going on. Jolie turned and looked at Marty and Tru; wrapped in each other's energy, their strength growing as their determination grew. If they had been a hundred feet apart, there would still have been no distance between them. And there was Sean, who seemed less and less the young man she knew, and more and more like an older man she knew much better, but could not place.

There you are, she greeted this other Sean, silently. He smiled back as if his older wiser self-recognized her from some other place and time as well.

Jolie looked down at the circle. The colored energies she saw around people were fading, but they had not gone out. Each fought the darkness, pushing it back in their own small way. They knew nothing and still they fought.

They're the brave ones, Jolie thought, feeling a sudden rush of admiration for the human race. The faint tracings of wispy wings could be seen behind some of the people, glowing arms wrapped around others, holding them so they would not fall. White star-like orbs shone in the foreheads of some of the ceremony attendees, while others pushed out pink and green energy from their hearts.

"When the ceremony began, the Light was called in. It's still here, but the spirits have no hands in the physical world. Someone here in this world must be their hands," the many spirit lights spoke inside Jolie as one voice.

The fire that the people had lit to symbolize the return of the light, flickered weakly. When it went out, they would be left in darkness.

"They gathered to celebrate The Return of the Light. Use that," the lights encouraged her.

Jolie shook her head. *"I don't know how."*

"You do. This is what you were born for; trust us."

I don't trust anyone, you lied to me. You said you'd be there and you weren't, a small voice inside Jolie wailed. But she knew it wasn't true anymore. There were friends standing beside her; friends who were willing to help her, even though they could not see what she saw.

Chapter Eighteen

They trusted her, and she trusted them. She would not let them down.

Rory had begun his third pass. The spiral was almost complete.

He must not finish it. Jolie began to run down the hill.

CHAPTER NINETEEN

"**W**e have to end this. Sean, break the circle. Tru, stop the music. We need to get them out of the trance," Jolie gave orders like a general. "Marty, Tru called you a Boy Scout. Prove it. Get that fire going."

Rory was beginning to turn his body. When he did the sand would fall and finish the spell.

Jolie launched herself across the circle, skidding through the lines like she was sliding into home plate. Her hands hit the dirt, grinding small rocks into her palms, hip, and thigh. The momentum slammed her into Rory, knocking him over like a bowling pin. The bowl flew out of his hand, and he fell with a grunt. Jolie jumped to her feet, feeling the wound from the dog bite pull and split open. It was not important. Landing as sure-footed as a cat, she swept one leg then the other through the black lines until they were only dirty smudges on the ground.

The music stopped. Sean was pulling people's hands apart, yanking them out of the trance. Marty was kneeling by the fire blowing on the embers, a handful of dried sticks in his hand. Dazed and dizzy, people began to stumble about. Some fell to their knees, others simply sat down on the ground looking confused.

Mickey's girls ran into their mother's arms while over their heads, Iris and Mickey blinked at each other. Claire and some of Rory's followers were vomiting. Mae, Rick, and more of Rory's pack lay on the ground barely conscious.

Rebecca stumbled toward Jolie, who threw her a smile of encouragement not having time for more.

Chapter Nineteen

Jolie faced Rory across the ruined spiral. The yellow of his eyes mirrored the creatures he had summoned.

"It's over. You're done," she announced firmly. "This gathering is dedicated to the Return Of The Light and you and your kind, don't belong."

"Not done," Rory wheezed, not even sounding like a man anymore. "A bargain was made. The price has not been paid."

"Whatever bargain was made, was not made here by these people," Jolie insisted. "If something is owed you'll have to take it from the guy who made the bargain. The one whose body you're using."

Rebecca had walked toward her friend and now stood at the edge of the group, her brows knit as she tried to make sense of what she was seeing with her logical mind. It wasn't working.

"What does he mean a bargain?" Sean demanded. "What was promised?"

"A life." The creature cocked its Rory-head sideways. "They promised a life, but we went away hungry last night."

"Last night when they came to Aunt Mae's house," Jolie explained.

"They, who?" Sean asked, his jaw tight.

"What's going on here?" Mae staggered into the middle of the group. Seeing Jolie, her eyes narrowed. "What is she still doing here, Rory?"

The creature inside Rory turned to Mae, his eyes narrowing. "Ask this one. She knows. A bargain was made."

Everyone looked at Mae.

"You made a bargain with these things, Aunt Mae? For what?" Sean demanded.

"For Faith," Jolie answered.

The creature looked at Jolie blankly. "A life," it repeated. The name meant nothing to him. To it, a life was a life. It didn't matter whose it was, only that the agreement was kept.

"Don't be ridiculous. I did nothing of the kind," Mae protested.

Sean shook his head. "I could understand someone disturbed like Rory but I can't believe that Aunt Mae would--"

"What did Rory promise you, Mae?" Jolie pressed the older woman.

Mae lifted her chin. Jolie could see she was struggling to answer, but she could not speak.

"Follow the pattern of the spell," Mem's voice whispered to Jolie. *"What she says first will be the truths that were used to weave it."*

"I need to move on," Mae said silently. "Faith is getting old. She suffers all the time. Dying would be a blessing for her."

"Do you hear the truths twisting?" Mem asked Jolie. *"Hear how he has fed the woman her own sorrow, transforming it to anger."*

"I'm a servant in my own house, taking care of her all the time. It's all about her; the coven, you, Sean, everything—it's always Faith. It's her they listen to. It's her they care about, not me--everyone except for Rory. When Rory came, things changed."

"I'll bet they did," Marty scoffed.

"He lied, Mae," Jolie said. "Whatever Rory told you, it was not true."

"Faith isn't strong enough to lead anymore," Mae kept on, ignoring Jolie. "I'm the head of the McBride clan now."

Chapter Nineteen

Sean stepped forward. "This isn't the middle ages. There is no clan, and I wouldn't follow you across the street."

"He said I could see Robert again! He promised." Mae began to tremble as the spell loosened its grip. "He knows ceremonies--Faith would never have agreed to it." She looked around desperate to explain. "Don't you see, when Robert was sick, Faith said she wished she could die in his place. I wished it too. Rory was going to grant both of us our wish."

"Nothing will bring your husband back, Mae," Jolie told her calmly. "What you said, in the beginning, was the only part of this that was true; you need to move on. Everything else was Rory twisting things to get you to help him."

"Please. I need Robert. I miss him so much." Mae broke down crying.

Rebecca came up by Jolie. "My God, Jolie, where did you find these people?"

Jolie gave her a sharp look. "Not now, Becca."

Iris stepped out and addressed the creature. "Whatever bargain was made, was between you and Rory. The rest of us had no part in it."

"But this, your overlord," the creature argued. "You owe him allegiance. You must fulfill his promise!"

"He is not and we owe him nothing. What has been taken...?"

"Was given willingly," the creature interrupted, uncertainty creeping into his eyes. Things were not going its way. Was there a code among its kind, a code that Rory had tried to sidestep?

"What has been taken," Iris repeated. "Is enough. You have no more business here, not with us. We cannot interfere with a contract willingly entered into, but you cannot take from us reparations for what he promised."

"So be it, human," the creature hissed as it shrank out of Rory's back.

Rory collapsed onto the ground, his arms and legs shaking and flopping violently, his eyes rolling up into the back of his head. Mae dropped to her knees beside him.

"Rory! Rory!" She reached out and was thrown back by an invisible force. Her eyes went blank and her face fell into slack folds. "Oh, my God. Oh, my God," she muttered over and over.

"We have to give him CPR or something" Marty tried to step in to help, but he too was pushed back by the energy force.

"You can't help him, Marty," Jolie said, softly. "No one can. They're taking him." When she blinked, she saw it all: the gruesome scene of Rory's devouring. She turned away and found her face nuzzled into Sean's chest. She tried not to close her eyes, but even with them open, she could feel Rory's life force being sucked away. Finally, the creatures began slinking back to whatever world it had been summoned from.

"Is he... Is he dead?" Tru asked in a small voice, staring at the pale, still body.

Rebecca looked almost as ghostly, but she had not flinched or fallen apart. There was more to her than Jolie had given her credit for.

Marty knelt beside Rory's body and felt for a pulse. This time nothing stopped him... "He's dead." He looked to Jolie as if he did not believe it. "What do we do?"

"We do what we would always do," Iris answered, prim-lipped. "Call 911." She pulled out her phone and punched in the numbers. "We have a medical emergency here."

Chapter Nineteen

The ceremony participants had regained a more normal state of consciousness and were saying their goodbyes, heading to their cars. Only a few had noticed that something unusual was going on in the center of the circle, fewer still stopped to see what it was. Tru and the coven ladies bunched themselves around the body to contain word getting out about the deadly turn of events.

Marty fetched a blanket from the RV and covered the body. "What should we say when they ask what happened?"

"Just say what you saw," Iris told him. "At the end of the ceremony, Rory collapsed. Leave the rest to the coroner." The others exchanged glances. No one disagreed. "The only one here who actually saw anything different was Jolie, right? And she's not talking to anybody tonight."

Jolie nodded. The adrenaline was beginning to ebb and she was starting to feel weak in the knees. It had been a long couple of days.

They were all standing there, lost in their own thoughts about the night's strange events, when Rick bulled his way into the circle.

"I thought I told you to stay in the truck," he barked at Jolie, not even noticing the blanketed mound.

"Guess I didn't listen, or just didn't give a shit." Her adrenaline was rising again, fast.

Rick's face went red. "I don't know what you think you're playing at, but someone needs to take you down a peg or two." He moved toward Jolie menacingly.

"Stop!" Jolie stretched her arm out toward him, her fingers wide.

Rick stumbled over his own feet as if they had suddenly refused to move.

"No more. Do you hear me? You will never come near me, or my mother, ever again," Jolie formed the words and the intent very carefully.

Rick sneered. "I don't take orders from little girls."

"I'm not a little girl. I'm a Boulet. So don't even think about messing with me, because you are no Simon Magus. You are a fake, I'm not. I'm the real thing; a Boulet and the Boulet's have a tradition of magic going back hundreds of years. It's in our blood, and you have no idea what we're capable of."

Rick's jaw went slack.

"I knew it!" Rebecca slapped her thigh. Jolie shot her another look. "Sorry, Jo."

A red police light flickered around the parking area. The officer got out of his car, checking out those who were leaving: the benign, the faux fey, and the out and out bizarre, who had come with Rory. Those who noticed the cop eyed him curiously, or suspiciously, or turned to avoid him, but no one approached him.

"Marty, go fetch the officer before he gets lost or eaten by the natives," Iris directed. "Jolie, take your friend and go to the RV. Are you sticking around for the explanations, Rick?"

Rick's eyes got big. He wasn't. Jolie watched him cower into the shadows making a wide circle around Marty and the approaching officer. If she was lucky, she would never see him again.

The confidence of the universe that had flown through her was fading. She was just herself again, Jolie Figg-Boulet, a confused girl, with more obstacles in her life than any kid should have, and less help than she deserved.

"Come on, Jo." Becca put an arm around Jolie's shoulders and led her to the RV. "I need to sit down."

Chapter Nineteen

By the time the Highway Patrol Officer was done asking questions, and the ambulance had taken Rory's body away, the stragglers had given up on the drama and headed back to town. Rebecca's friends had taken her home with them, and except for Mae, who had been put to bed in the RV in a state of shock, the coven ladies were all that was left. Mickey and her girls were finishing uploading their car. Sean was checking to be sure everything in the RV was battened down and ready to travel, and Iris was saying good night to Claire, complete with reassuring hugs and homilies about living every day to the max because you just never knew how long you had.

Jolie sat alone on a rock, hugging herself against the cold, and wondering what she was supposed to be feeling about all this. Someone had died, but she didn't feel sad. She'd won a battle, but she didn't feel triumphant. She'd faced demons, but she didn't feel scared, and Sean had kissed her, but she didn't feel giddy. Mostly, she felt everything all at once and at fifteen, it was a little overwhelming.

An unmarked car pulled in and Cliff Wrangler climbed out of it.

Jolie groaned. "Crap. What's he doing here?"

Wrangler looked around, spied Jolie, and came ambling toward her, his cowboy hat pulled down low.

"Good evening, Miss Figg."

"Officer Cliff. What are you doing all the way out here?"

"Funny, I was about to ask you the same thing."

"I came for the festivities, but it didn't turn out too festive."

"I heard. A dead body tends to dampen the holiday mood. A friend of yours?"

Jolie shook her head. "No, just some guy my mom's boyfriend knew."

"Rick? Is he around?"

"No. He split a while ago, I think."

"Is that who you came with?"

"Yeah, sort of."

"You know your mother turned you in as a runaway."

"What? Why'd she do that?" Jolie felt like a bug under a microscope the way he was studying her.

"She did say it was possible you'd been taken against your will. That's kidnapping, you know. Is that what happened?"

Jolie's eyes shifted nervously. What could she say? That was exactly what happened, but Jessie Lynn had said she should go with Rick before they argued, so technically he had her mom's permission.

"Jolie?" Wrangler prodded.

"Not exactly," Jolie answered, reluctantly.

"Okay, but he dumped you. You do understand that, right? He's not a good guy. He's a jerk. Older guys may seem cool and exciting, but there's a reason there's laws against them getting involved with younger girls."

Jolie stared at him. *He thinks I'm into Rick.* She wanted to throw up

"It's not like that," she protested.

"It never is," Wrangler said, sarcastically. Iris came striding towards them.

"Hello. I'm Iris Fadgeon, one of the organizers of the event. Can I help you with something?" She placed herself firmly by Jolie's side.

"Officer Wrangler," Cliff held out his hand and shook Iris'. "Tough night , huh?"

"Tragic. We're all in shock. We've already given our statements, though, so is there something else I need

Chapter Nineteen

to help you with? We're just about finished up here and looking forward to getting home."

"Officer Cliff's a Probation guy, Iris," Jolie explained. "He's here for me."

"For you? I don't understand, Jo. You didn't have anything to do with any of this."

"Apparently Mom came home and freaked out when I wasn't there. Thought I'd run away, or got kidnapped, or some stupid thing."

"Oh dear." Iris turned to Wrangler. "I'm afraid this is my fault. Jessie was supposed to bring Jolie tonight, but she got called into work, so we had a friend of Rory's pick Jo up. With everything so crazy, I didn't think to ask if she'd left a note or anything, but she's been here under my supervision all night. I'm responsible for her."

Wrangler examined the diminutive fashion plate with her snow white hair, Dior pantsuit, and straightforward manner.

"So you'll be taking her home then, yourself, Ma'am?"

"That was the plan. She would have been back hours ago except, well, you understand. Under the circumstances, I couldn't leave. I'll speak to Jolie's mother and apologize for any misunderstanding. I'm sure we'll get it all sorted out without any further inconvenience to your department."

"I'm sure." If Wrangler realized he was being snowed, he was too much of a gentleman to mention it. He tipped his hat. "Well then, I'll be off. Good night, ladies."

"Good save, Iris," Jolie said as he walked away. "I owe you one."

Iris shook her head. "Not even close. It's us who owe you. What you did tonight, Jolie, we can't ever repay."

Sean came out of the RV waving to Mickey as she pulled out. Even the inner circle were leaving. Tru and Marty were headed back toward Jolie. She smiled. She'd known they wouldn't leave without making sure she was all right. She liked that. It felt like someone cared.

The five of them converged on the abandoned ceremonial grounds looking tired and pensive.

"It feels different now," Tru said sadly.

Iris nodded. "We'll probably have to look for a new place to hold the ceremony next year."

"Do you really think people will come again, once they know what happened?" Marty looked skeptical.

"Are you kidding? People love this stuff," Iris teased, flipping her hand, and slipping into a full-blown New York accent.

"Well, you can count me out," Jolie said, firmly. "I'm done with all this magic shit. I'm going to go back to school and be a normal kid in a normal world."

The others looked at each other and started to laugh.

"What'd I say?"

"Nothing." Sean's eyes sparkled with good humor.

"I mean it. I'm not a witch," she insisted. "I'm not a medium. I'm not a psychic. I'm just me."

"That's good enough for us, kid." Marty grinned.

A sliver of warmth slowly spread over the hills.

"Look, it's dawn," Tru said, softly, snuggling closer to Marty.

"A new day," Iris added.

"A new year." Sean put his jacket around Jolie's shoulders.

"The Light has returned," Iris whispered the ceremonial words.

Chapter Nineteen

"The Light has returned," Tru echoed.
Once again the darkness had been pushed back.

CHAPTER TWENTY

Jolie sat in front of the trailer, wrapped in the warmth of Sean's jacket. It smelled like cologne, gasoline, and incense. The winter sun warmed her face, feeling like a special gift. Just living felt like a special gift. Okay, maybe it wasn't perfect; the fit was a little tight here and there, but it was a gift nevertheless, one that with a little patience and determination, Jolie was beginning to think she could shape it to fit her.

Betty hobbled out of a shed three trailers away rubbing the sleep from her eyes, and when she saw Jolie, she came over.

"Nice morning," she croaked.

"Morning? Heck, it's after ten o'clock. It's almost lunch time," Jolie teased her.

Betty grinned. "I must have slept through the morning traffic report. A guy I know who goes to the dump a lot made me a special box with some weird stuff inside that he said would stop the radio waves. I think it worked."

"Yeah?"

"Taking out the fillings would probably be better, though. You know, I was thinking, it's a few days before Christmas; maybe I ought to call my family. I mean, even if they don't want to see me, it might be good to let them know I'm alive."

Jolie stood up. "I think that's a great idea, Betty. You can use our phone inside where it's warm if you want. Mom's in there, but she won't mind."

The old woman hesitated. "What about Rick?"

"You don't have to worry about Rick. I don't think he'll be coming around anymore." Jolie opened the trailer door. "Mom, Betty's coming in to borrow the phone, okay?"

"You're a good kid, Jolie. Don't let anyone tell you different." The old woman smiled as she went inside.

Sean drove in on his motorcycle, wearing an old army surplus jacket, and a knitted beanie. He rolled up in front of Jolie and stopped, leaving the motor idling.

"Hey, you."

"Hey."

"How are you doing?"

"Okay. You?"

Sean nodded. "I thought I'd go see Faith before she checks out this morning. She's gonna stay at Iris's a few days, then she's talking about getting a place of her own, and having someone come in to help out a few hours a week. Didn't you say you were looking for a part time job?"

"I didn't, but I would. What about Mae? What's going to happen to her?"

"It'd be pretty hard to explain what she was guilty of."

"So she gets off Scot free?"

"She's lost the trust of the family and the coven on top of losing Uncle Robert; that's hardly getting off free, and there were mitigating circumstances."

"Mitigating? Wow, that's a big word for a biker guy." Jolie smiled. "Thanks for the coat." She took off the jacket and held it out to him.

"It's okay. Keep it."

"Really?"

"Sure."

"It wouldn't mean we were going steady or anything, would it?"

"No. It would mean I trusted you with my jacket until you got a decent one of your own."

Jolie grinned. "Cool. You know my mom's a cocktail waitress, so it could be awhile."

"That's okay. So, do you want to come with me to see Faith?"

Jolie studied him, looking for that older Sean that was him and somehow not him yet, or anymore. He was there, somewhere, lingering in the future, or the past.

"Stop looking at me like that," Sean said.

"Like what?" She demanded.

"Like I'm some biology experiment and you're trying to figure out where to make the first cut."

"I got a D in biology."

"Even scarier."

Jolie shook her head. Something had changed between them. They had known each other for only a few months, and yet, she was sure they had been connected for a long time before that. What would that mean to them now in this life? She didn't know, but she did know that whatever their relationship turned out to be, it would be based on more than simple biology.

"So, are you coming or not?" Sean prodded.

"I'm thinking about it."

"How hard do you have to think? It's a simple question."

"No, it's not. It's complicated, and it's going to take some time for me to figure it all out."

"Do you think you could take time out from your busy journey of self-discovery to have Christmas dinner with Faith, and Iris, and me? Your mom's invited, too, of course."

"Yeah. I'd like that."

"Cool. So now get on, or I'm leaving without you."

Chapter Twenty

"Douche bag." Jolie opened the trailer door. Jessie Lynn and Betty were sitting at the dinette drinking coffee. "Mom, Sean's taking me to see Faith. I'll be back in a few hours."

"Have you got your key?" Jessie Lynn asked.

Jolie grabbed her key off the peg at the side of the door and let it swing in the sunshine.

"New year, new world, new key." She dangled it in front of Sean. "Got the locks changed this morning." She climbed onto the back of the bike and wrapped her arms around Sean's waist.

In a week, she'd be back in school with Becca and the rest of it; kids and teachers, tests and homework, judgment, drama, and all the bizarre injustices of high school hierarchies. After this winter break, it was going to feel like a friggin' vacation.

Watch for:

GHOSTS IN THE GRAVEYARD
Book Two of
THE JOLIE CHRONICLES

by E.F. Winters
Copyright©2015 by E.F.Winters

Bumped hard from behind, Jolie Figg fell forward.

"Hey! Watch it," she barked as she caught herself, her books flying from her arms.

Proving her theory of the fickle nature of reality, the books went slow-mo, hanging, suspended mid-air like birds struggling to fly into the face of a storm. Vision replaced reality. The school hallway disappeared.

Car brakes screeched. Metal slammed against metal and a battered yellow skateboard corkscrewed into the blue sky in a futile bid for freedom. Gravity pulled it back down into the mess of the car accident below.

Jolie's vision broke as the board shattered against the pavement, her books thudding onto the floor and sliding away in three directions.

"Sorry," a dark haired boy shouted over his shoulder. "I'm late for class."

"Jerk," Jolie muttered as she tried to retrieve her books, dodging between semi-truck football players and smaller sportier student models.

Her Biology book became a hockey puck.

"Score," the muscle-bound jock leered. "Oh, was that yours, Witch Girl?" His entourage laughed, celebrating with high fives.

"Surfs up!" English Two got a new life as a surfboard, while Geometry raced toward the stairwell, saved from a dead drop by striking the corner post.

The vision of a crash swirled through Jolie's mind, fogging out the scene in the hallway. The hard, cold surfaces of a hospital room replaced it.

No. Jolie gritted her teeth, pushing the vision away.

She hated this. She was always careful not to touch anybody, walking with her head down to avoid eye contact, keeping to herself. The last thing she wanted, was to be burdened by her peer's stupid secrets. But it wasn't enough anymore. Things were changing. Her ability to hear other people's thoughts was becoming harder to avoid. It wasn't fair. How could someone who didn't want to be psychic become more psychic? She didn't want to know these things about other people and their rotten lives. She didn't want to get involved in their problems. With a mom who treated everything in her own life like it was disposable, including her daughter, Jolie had enough problems of her own. Her friend and mentor, Faith was helping Jolie learn to work with her gifts, but the visions and headaches that had begun to accompany her psychic disability were getting more intense.

Once again the vision won and the fog of someone else's life enveloped the gifted teenager.

The image of a young man covered with abrasions bloomed in Jolie's mind. An oxygen mask covered most of his face, the tubes sprouted from his body making him look like a medical Chia pet.

"Get out of my head," Jolie demanded, grabbing at reality. *"This has nothing to do with me."*

A pale blond Brady Bunch mom stood by the boy's bed with one arm around a younger version of herself.

The mom and the sister, Jolie thought, though something seemed not quite right about that. If the boy was part of this family, someone had colored him with the wrong crayons.